Feo Belcari

The life of B. Giov. Colombini

Translated from the Editions of 1541and 1832

Feo Belcari

The life of B. Giov. Colombini
Translated from the Editions of 1541and 1832

ISBN/EAN: 9783741192968

Manufactured in Europe, USA, Canada, Australia, Japa

Cover: Foto ©Andreas Hilbeck / pixelio.de

Manufactured and distributed by brebook publishing software
(www.brebook.com)

Feo Belcari

The life of B. Giov. Colombini

CONTENTS.

—◦◦—

B. GIOVANNI COLOMBINI.

CHAPTER I.

The Country and Parentage of Giovanni.

ERE begins the venerable and holy life of the Blessed Giovanni Colombini, who was the first of the poor ones called, for the sake of Jesus Christ, Gesuati.

The ancient and famous city of Siena, as she has beyond any other countries had a most singular reverence and devotion to the Mother of God, so she has been a most fruitful mother of good servants of God; and, amongst other holy men to whom she has given birth, was one by name and by grace called Giovanni, of the honourable house of Colombini, who, much in accordance with the simplicity and purity of his heart, was surnamed Colombino. His father was called Pietro, and his mother Agnolina. This gentleman was rich in temporal blessings, and no less so in honourable relations; and amongst the chiefs of the city he was in such repute that, raised to the post of governor of the city with the other good and wise citizens, he many times wisely ruled it.

His lawful wife was Mona Biagia, daughter of Messer Giovanni, whose father was Messer Niccolo (both knights of the noble family of Cerrétani), a venerable and honourable lady, and well brought up in all the approved manners; and by her he had two children, a boy and a girl, to whom he gave his parents' names, that is, to the boy, Pietro, to the girl, Agnolina. He was much given to earthly gains, and always anxious about his business, prudent and circumspect in all secular affairs. But the good and merciful God, wishing to draw this man to Himself and free him from the power of darkness, converted him in the manner hereinafter written.

CHAPTER II.

His Conversion.

ONE day, A.D. 1355, Giovanni having returned home, wishing to dine at once, and not finding the table and meal prepared, as was usual, he began to be angry with his wife and servant, reproving them for their delay, alleging that for urgent reasons he was most anxious to return to his business; to which his wife, gently replying, said, "Thou hast too much gain, and little expenditure; why dost thou worry thyself so much?" And she prayed him to be patient, that he should very soon have something to eat. She also said, "While I prepare the meal, take this book and read a little;" putting before him a volume which contained some lives of saints. But Giovanni, offended, took the book, and throwing it into the middle of the room, said to her, "Thou thinkest of nothing but legends, and I must very soon return to the warehouse."

2 *

While saying these and many other words, his conscience began to prick him, so that he picked up the
book from the ground, and sat down ; and having
opened it, there came before him, by God's will, the
life of S. Marie of Egypt, a.sinner converted by God
to marvellous piety.

While Giovanni read this his wife prepared the
dinner, and desired him, when he pleased, to sit down
to table.   Giovanni answered her, " *Thou* must wait
a little now, till I have read this legend ;" which
happened to be of some length, and because it was
full of heavenly melody, his heart began to soften,
and he would not leave off reading till he had come
to the end.   His wife, seeing him read so attentively,
and silently considering it, was much rejoiced, hoping
that he would enjoy it to the edification of his soul,
for it was not his custom to read such books.   And
certain it is, that by the operation of the Divine
grace it so fell out, for that history so impressed
itself on his soul, that he continually meditated on it
day and night.   And with his thoughts thus fixed,
the gracious God so touched his heart, that he began
to despise the things of this world, and to be no
longer so anxious about them as he used, but rather
the contrary ; for at first he was so avaricious that

he rarely gave alms himself, or liked any one in his
house to do so, and out of covetousness he tried
in his payments to deduct something from the agree-
ment made ; but after the aforesaid salutary lesson,
to punish himself for his avarice, he often gave twice
as much as was demanded of him, and to those who
sold him anything, he paid more money than was
due.   And so he began to frequent the churches, to
fast often, and to give himself up to prayer and other
devout acts.

CHAPTER III.

How the Blessed John made a Vow of Chastity.

N this way, chastising the flesh and bringing it into subjection, he wished to live in chastity; and with many reasons and examples he exhorted his wife that she should willingly abandon every carnal action and live holily; who, consenting to the holy desire of her husband, though she was young, they both determined and firmly resolved to keep chastity till death; and directly this resolution was made the true-hearted Giovanni knelt down in presence of his wife, and courageously said, "O Lord Jesus Christ, as my wife is willing to observe chastity, so I promise thee to observe it as long as I live." And from that hour he began no longer to lie down in bed, sleeping sometimes on a box, and sometimes on a bench, watching great part of the night in prayer. And having been occupied in such works for some time, growing in virtue, and daily improving in the way of the Lord, giving large alms to the poor, he began to wish to be entirely poor and a mendicant for the love of Jesus Christ, so that, deprived of all, and of every earthly care, he could diligently follow the poor Christ, his Lord. And then he began to despise himself in the sight of others, and to go meanly clad.

CHAPTER IV.

Francesco Vincenti joins him.

ONTINUING this life, it happened that he met one of his friends and companions who was called Francesco, the son of Mino de Vincenti, a man held in honour, and one of the chief men of the same city, to whom he revealed the secret of his heart, *i.e.*, how he wished to be utterly poor out of love to Jesus Christ, begging and praying him to do the like ; and after often talking together, and speaking much of God and of contempt of the world, Francesco resolved to be of one mind with Giovanni in everything; and being so far mutually agreed, they began, for the love of Jesus Christ, to distribute largely amongst the poor those riches which they formerly used to heap up with much avarice and eagerness, and Francesco began to go meanly clad like Giovanni, determining to follow him in manner and in everything. The people of the country spoke

much of this novelty, for they all wondered at such
a marvellous change; and certainly they might mar-
vel at seeing these very diligent patricians of their
city, so abounding in earthly riches, despise and hold
in contempt with such fervour their own selves, their
substance, and all earthly things. And whilst they
were leading this sort of life, it happened that at
one time the new knight of Christ, Giovanni, being
sick, and seeing that he received many kind atten-
tions from his wife and the aforesaid Francesco, from
the desire of poverty he rose from his bed, put a
blanket over his shoulders, and went secretly to the
hospital for the poor in Siena. His wife and
Francesco entered his room, and not finding him they
marvelled much. Then they went about seeking for
him amongst relations and friends, and could not
find him; at last, searching the hospitals, they found
him in the very poorest, and said to him, "Why
hast thou fled in this way, for we have been nearly
two days looking for thee?" Giovanni replied, "I
am happy, and you will not let me stay because
this lady of the hospital wished me soon to cook a
potage of leaves." But at last, not to grieve them
any further, he returned home with them.

CHAPTER V.

A Marvellous Light seen in Giovanni's Chamber.   He gives more Alms, in opposition to his Wife.

GAIN, while the devout servant of God lived in his own house, it happened that Mona Alessa, of the noble race of Bandinelli, wife of Spinello, son of Messer Niccolo Cerretani, having come to spend a few days with Giovanni's wife, one night before she went to bed she saw Giovanni's room full of a marvellous light, and not thinking that he was there, on going in to know the reason, she found him kneeling at prayer, without any other natural or artificial light; therefore, having perceived without doubt that that extraordinary light came from God, she, silently, and without making any noise, and full of wonder, left the room.

And thus leading a holy life, after a little time Giovanni's son, having reached the age of twelve years, passed from this mortal life, for which death

Giovanni gave God thanks, congratulated himself, and received great consolation, seeing that he was left more free, and at liberty to devote his wealth to God; and so he did, for from this time he began to give alms often, and still more often to bring poor beggars to his house, giving them food, washing their feet, and re-clothing them.

Now Giovanni's wife, seeing that he thought so little of himself, and gave so largely of his wealth to the poor, although she was, as we have said, religiously disposed, still, as she was not so enamoured of poverty, she bore his great compassion impatiently; and advising him, under colour of temperance and discretion in the great fervour and action of his spirit, she tried with prayers to convince him; but he gently answered her, "Thou prayedst to God that I might become charitable, and give myself to virtue, and for this thou also prayedst to His servants; and now thou art vexed that I make a little amends for my avarice and my other sins." His wife made him this reply, "I prayed that it might rain, but not that a deluge should come." And Giovanni affirmed that every one was in a dream and raving, and that human life was like smoke, and a wind that passes away; and that he who has gathered most riches has the worst bargain.

And he added, we should think of the life in heaven,
which will be everlasting, which one can acquire with
little fatigue, and also that the greater the pains
which we suffer for Christ, so much greater are the
consolations which we receive for those pains; because to every one who, out of love to Christ, will
leave riches and honours, He will give such a ful-
ness of sweetness and comfort to the soul, that it
will say, "I refuse every delight which a hundred
worlds would give me." And with many other words
he tried to persuade her to be willing that he should
follow Christ in extreme poverty; and many times he
earnestly implored her to give him leave, and by her
consent free him from the laws of matrimony, so
that, released from every earthly care, he could more
easily devote himself to God, and walk in the way of
His good and holy vocation; but in no way did she
consent to set him free.

CHAPTER VI.

What happened to Giovanni and Francesco about a Leper.

NOW it happened one day that the servants of God, Giovanni and Francesco, when going to hear Mass at the Duomo, saw at the door of the church, amongst the other poor creatures who were begging there, a man sick with leprosy, and half naked, who was covered from head to foot with scabs and sores. Giovanni seeing him, and moved in his inmost heart to pity and compassion, said to Francesco, "Look at this poor creature here, deprived of every human aid. Shall we take him home, and for love of Christ take care of him? We were about to *hear* Mass; this will be to *do* it." Francesco replied, "Do what thou wilt." Then this despised Giovanni embraced that leper, and lifted him on to a bench, and put his head between his thighs, and so bore him on his shoulders in triumph, holding the leper's hand in his, and with a sweet charity he gently laid his cheeks on those corrupt and wounded thighs, first on one, then on the other; and on arriving at the house they brought him in. But when Giovanni's wife saw him, disgusted and horrified at the ghastly disease, she said at once, "Are these the goods that thou bringest to me? Hast thou brought me home corruption and rottenness? I will leave the house, and thou canst do thy pleasure, as thou art wont." But Giovanni gently answered her, saying, "I pray thee to have patience. This is one of God's creatures, redeemed as we are by His precious Blood, and we *might* become like him, if God willed it. For the love of Christ, I pray thee allow me to put him in our bed, so that he may rest awhile. Oh, remember how many pleasures we have had, and how many sins we have committed, and offended our Creator. Don't let it trouble thee to make some little amends for them; know that the poor and the sick represent the person of Christ, because He says in the Holy Gospel, 'Whenever you remember and do good to one of these My least ones, you do it unto Me.'" She replied, "Thou hast plenty to say, do as thou wilt; I will not meddle in it, and if you put him into our bed, I will never lie there again. Dost thou not now perceive and smell the stink he gives forth? I can bear it no longer." Then Giovanni and Francesco, not heeding the lady's words, having prepared a tepid bath, carefully washed the leper all over; and after they had gently dried him, they laid him to rest awhile in the best bed, where the lady was accustomed to lie, at which she was displeased. Finally, Giovanni, that he might mortify himself still further for the love of Christ, drank some of the same water with which they had washed the leper, and afterwards admonished his wife, that before they should return from church, she should sometimes visit the sick man; and with his companion, Francesco, he returned to hear Mass. But she did not promise to do this: nevertheless, beginning to be stung by the pricks of conscience, because she did not fulfil her husband's commands, and was not moved to pity for the invalid, rising up, she went to the leper, and when she opened the door of the room, she smelt such a very sweet fragrant smell, as if all sorts of spices and sweet scented things were gathered there. For which reason, not daring to enter, she shut the door, and began to weep bitter tears of repentance, thinking specially of the words she had spoken to her husband about that poor sick man. At this moment Giovanni and Francesco

returned from church, having on the way bought
confections for the relief of the sick man. And directly
they entered the house, Giovanni said to his wife,
" Why weepest thou ? and what news of our invalid ?"
to whom replying with many tears, she narrated what
had happened to her on going there ; on understanding which the servants of God ran to the room, and
on opening the door smelt that same sweet fragrance,
and uncovering the bed, they found no one there.
Then they knew it had been Jesus Christ who had
shown Himself to them in the form of a leper ; and
perceiving such a great gift of God, they returned
Him most hearty thanks. But Giovanni, the servant
of God, anxious only to please Christ, strictly commanded his wife to tell this to no one as long as she
lived ; and she, having seen the great sign which God
had shown, gave her husband full liberty, and entirely
loosed him from the bonds of matrimony, and set him
free ; and said to him, " Go or stay, just as it pleases
thee, and give what thou wilt for God ; for I will never
again oppose thee in anything thou wouldest do."
Giovanni, much rejoiced at this permission, gave
thanks for it to the Author of all good.

Then Giovanni and Francesco, still more kindled
by the Divine fire, wishing to give up the world en-

tirely, and not being sure of their own judgment, sought for good advice as to the way and manner of life they were about to lead, and prayed much, and decided on being advised by religious people on the best course to take.

CHAPTER VII.

How they take Counsel with some good Servants of God,
and resolve to Live in Poverty.

AT that time there were living in Siena some
good and enlightened servants of God, of
great holiness, among whom were Don Pietro dè
Petroni, of the same country, a man of much
thought, and of holy life and doctrine. Of this man
and many others, Giovanni sought for advice as to
the best way of following Jesus Christ, and all agreed
in saying that the shortest and most direct way was
through the meanest and most abject poverty, which
is the least open to the praise of men, and most
hidden from the opinion of the vulgar. He also
consulted many masters of sacred theology, who all
agreed in this, affirming that abject poverty had been
the way of the Saviour Jesus Christ, who called and
said, " Let him who will be my servant follow me."
Then the servants of Christ listened with greater confidence to the very wholesome advice of their spiritual

friends, when they perceived that it was confirmed by the voice of the great counsellor Jesus Christ, Who having shown the necessary way of the commandments to the young man who had asked Him, and wishing to give him the highest rule of life, added directly the perfection of His counsel, saying, "If thou wilt be perfect, go sell what thou hast, and give to the poor, and come follow me." Then having taken counsel of the great Master Christ, and having determined on following Him in the way of abject poverty, there remaining to Giovanni a girl of thirteen years of age, and to Francesco another of five years, both legitimate and natural, they mutually agreed to put them into one of the best convents of venerable and honourable ladies of the Benedictine Order, dedicated to SS. Abundio and Abundanzio, vulgarly called Santa Bonda, about half a mile from Siena, and in the year of our Lord 1363 they put those children into that convent. Giovanni divided his possessions into three parts: one part he gave to the above-mentioned Convent of Santa Bonda, one to the great Hospital of Siena, and another to the sisterhood of the Virgin Mary, on condition that the convent and the sisterhood should each be bound to give annually a certain sum of money to his wife, also some articles of food for her sustenance, and a maid to wait upon her; and this he did with his wife's consent because of his gifts. His other goods he had already distributed to the poor, for some time before he had given up his traffic in the sale of cloth goods and other merchandise, which he had carried on in Siena and Perugia and other places, and had given up everything for God; for when he was converted to Christ he possessed about 1200 florins. Francesco gave, for the love of God, all his goods, both movable and immovable, to the same monastery, on condition that the Abbess would receive into it, for God's love, six poor girls, without any dowry, to become nuns. And he offered up his daughter on the altar of this convent; and to make his alms perfect, he also offered up himself, vowing perpetual chastity, poverty, and obedience to the Abbess, saying, "I thank God, who has given me grace to offer to Him all my wealth and my own self. I wish that the convent should not be bound to give me even a piece of bread, but as alms are given to the rest of the poor;" and he wished this to be set down in writing by the hand of the public notary, so that every one then present was moved to tears.

CHAPTER VIII.

Wonderful Mortifications of the Servants of God,
Giovanni and Francesco.

THUS the brave soldiers of Christ, having become new spouses of extreme poverty, gladly began to beg, asking for bread and wine for the love of God, and were raised in this way to a great height of love, treading the world under their feet, and esteeming every earthly thing as dust, and increasing every day in the desire of suffering and bearing pain out of love to Christ. For the love of Him they esteemed hunger, thirst, cold, nakedness, great inconveniences, oppressions, reproaches, and all the railing of the world, as pleasure and ease. Indeed it was a wonderful thing to see men, who were much respected, and by the world thought prudent and circumspect, now having made themselves fools that they might become wise. For whereas the man of God, Giovanni, before he became poor, was richly dressed in clothes dyed in

fine colours, and in winter wore under his doublet
a lining of the finest fur, with a hood over his head,
gloves lined, and sometimes two pairs of hose, one
over the other, as well as socks and shoes; and
used to eat by the fire, using fine and delicately-pre-
pared food; with all that often suffering pains of the
stomach, weariness, headache, and other infirmities.
Now, warmed by the Divine fire, forsaking every
luxury and care of the flesh, he went unshod, wearing nothing on his head, clad in a scanty robe, with
a short cloak of rough coarse cloth, and that patched ;
he took food roughly prepared, and nevertheless he
was cured of every infirmity, and freed from his
accustomed pains ; and because of the love which
burnt in his breast, he was so kindled with heat,
that cold was driven away from his body; whence,
also, the few clothes that he wore were left unbuttoned over his chest. All which things one of
his friends observing, asked him one day, saying,
" Art thou not cold, Giovanni ? " To which he
replied, " Give me thy hand," and taking his hand,
he put it into his bosom, saying, " Does it seem to
thee that I am cold ? " His friend answered, " No,
surely, rather thou art so hot that I can no longer
bear my hand there."

Thus then the good servants of God, living poorly and meanly, gave themselves up to mortifications whenever they could. Therefore, that they might follow the steps of their Lord Jesus Christ, they determined on receiving dishonour where they had received honour: for having held high office amongst the nine chief men of the city, and remembering the honour and reverence which had been paid them for two months, they wished to be abased for the same period, and in the same palace, and to perform the meanest services. As there was yet no fountain in the palace, they brought all the water that was wanted from the well in the field, and also carried the firewood upstairs; they turned the roasts in the kitchen, they washed the pots and the pans and other necessary things; they swept the halls and the piazza in front of the palace, and did all the lowest offices; and for these two months, when they had become for the love of God the lowest servants of the cook, they would not have meat or drink in the palace, but begged for their food in the streets. Also in the country round they humbled themselves, going to the houses of the dead, bearing the tapers to the Church, burying the dead bodies, and doing similar offices; and when out of reverence it was denied to them, they begged that for the love of Christ that spiritual gain might not be taken from them. And all these things they did without any reward, that they might avenge themselves for the honours they had received in their own country.

And in such mortifications they were by some laughed at and held in scorn, and by some commended and had in reverence. But they never listened to what was said of them, either in praise or blame, but were all the more anxious for the salvation of their own and their neighbours' souls. Only once, when the man of God, Giovanni, wishing to avenge himself for the pomp with which he had ridden through the city, mounted an ass, and going round the market-place, certain merchants who were at their warehouses, seeing him going in this manner, began by words and actions to deride him; to whom Giovanni, with a joyful look, replied, "You laugh at me, and I at you," as if he would say, "You despise me because I follow Christ, and I despise you because you follow the world."

CHAPTER IX

How they Received Novices into their Poor Society.

AND in such severe living Giovanni and Francesco served God two years or more, from the day they began to beg, without any other companions. But their holiness, like a city set on a hill or a light on a candlestick, could not long be hid; for many, having seen the honours and riches which Giovanni and Francesco had renounced, and the misery and poverty which they had embraced for the love of Christ, attracted by the odour of their virtues, had such great reverence and love for them, that by their example and teaching they left off sin and vices, and gave themselves up to holy works and good living. Some, renouncing the world, became religious, and many, remaining in their houses, lived virtuously, amending their lives. Many citizens also, who wished perfectly to serve Christ, joined Francesco and Giovanni, really left the world, and became, together with them, lovers of abject poverty. And so these men of God went about the city, praising the Name of Jesus Christ with loud voices, affectionately exhorting sinners to turn to repentance.

CHAPTER X

Conversion of the Son of Niccolò di Nerdusa.

HE son of Niccolò di Nerdusa, of Siena, a young man above twenty years old, came one day to Giovanni, the servant of God, and told him that he was very anxious to become one of his spiritual children, adding that he would do whatever he wished; so Giovanni, wishing to see if he was really in earnest, told him that he should strip and re-clothe him at the public fountain. The young man replied that he might do what he would with him, as if he were a dead body. So Giovanni and his companions went to the market-place, and after first kneeling before the image of our Lady, they went to the fountain, where Giovanni ordered certain young men to pull off the youth's shoes and stockings; then they returned to the image of our Lady, and stripped him of his clothes, and put other very shabby garments on him. Whilst this was going on, Giovanni

and one of his companions called Il Boccia, sang a
devout hymn, beginning: "Diletto Jesù Cristo, chi
ben t'ama;"* and then they led him to the Duomo.
This sight brought many people 'together, as usually
happens on such occasions; and in this way they
inflicted great mortifications on the young man, for
Christ's sake.　He said afterwards that the suffering of death could not be worse than what he had
then endured; but the good Jesus rewarded him,
for the following night God came to him with such
power that he could not sleep for excessive joy.　God
worked great wonders in him, and revealed great
things to him, at which, when he related them,
those who heard him were astonished.　He earnestly
exhorted Giovanni and his brothers to preach Jesus
Christ, saying that the time was come when God
would show great mercy to sinners, and that Jesus
Christ had said to him: " Tell people that if they will
truly confess and repent of their sins, and faithfully
call on my Name, they shall see what I will do for
them."　After having received great spiritual consolations, the young man was deeply imbued with
the love of Christ, and going with Giovanni to the
convent of Santa Bonda, he spoke to the Abbess on

* " The beloved Jesus Christ, Who loves thee much."

behalf of Christ, saying, "It has been revealed to me by Christ that I owe this favour to your prayers, and that we should pray for people, for our prayers will be heard, and all are precious in God's sight;" and other wonderful things he related. He spoke so earnestly that the Abbess said to him: " Tell me, if thou lovest Christ so much as thou sayest, what wilt thou do for His sake?" The young man replied, "I would do anything that I was told." Then the Abbess said, "Go and strip thyself, and walk through Siena, proclaiming the Name of Jesus Christ." She said this to see if he really meant what he said. He at once took off his clothes and went out, but the Abbess told Giovanni to go and meet him, and bring him back. When the man of God (Giovanni) was writing an account of this to his friend, brother Giorgio, of San Domenico, who was then preaching at Volterra, he said to him, " Now you see how Christ blesses the man who really gives himself to Him, for in one day He can cause sinners and worldly-minded men to acquire the grace of perfection."

CHAPTER XI.

The Conversion of Tommaso Guelfaccio.

I MUST not omit to mention the wonderful conversion of Tommaso de Guelfaccio. This man was a citizen of Siena, of a noble family, one of the nine rulers, but was given to gluttony and every sensual and worldly pleasure. He hated all religions, especially this poor confraternity. One day, however, when Giovanni was going out of the city with some of his poor brothers, to visit his loved Convent of Santa Bonda, Tommaso followed him for his amusement; and when Giovanni came to a place where three roads met, and where a great cross of wood was erected, he looked behind, and seeing Tommaso, said to him, "Oh, Tommaso, wilt thou do me a favour, for Christ's sake?" Tommaso answered, "If I can I will gladly do it for you." "I pray thee," said Giovanni, "for Jesus Christ's sake, to kneel down at the foot of this cross and say a Paternoster and an Ave Maria." Tom-

maso said, "If that is all thou requirest, I will willingly
say not one only, but two." Giovanni replied, "I do
not want anything else of thee." Then Tommaso,
uncovering his head, knelt down and began to say
the Paternoster. The loving Giovanni also knelt
down and prayed earnestly that God would enlighten
Tommaso with His truth, and warm his heart with
His love. After Giovanni had spent some time in
prayers he rose up, when Tommaso threw himself at
his feet, imploring his pardon, and saying, "I will
not go until thou hast accepted me as one of the
least in thy holy company;" and thus miraculously
converted, he cast off his clothes, and dressed himself
meanly like the others, and so was received into the
poor congregation. All the city marvelled at this
conversion, and many thought he would not persevere; and Giovanni, the man of God, that brave
soldier of Christ, who fought so valiantly for His
honour, exhorted him earnestly, saying, "Remember,
dear brother, how thou hast laboured for the wicked
world, and now seek that Jesus Christ our Lord may
employ thee to His honour and glory. Know that in
proportion to thy faith and holy desire so will God
fill thy mind with goodness; therefore be brave, and
seek and strive for the honour of Jesus Christ." Tom-

maso fought victoriously against the world, the flesh, and the devil, and went barefoot and bareheaded, like the other poor brothers. One day a lay brother, begging for his convent, seeing that Tommaso, who had very often ridiculed him, had a hard black substance on his head, said to him in joke, "Tommaso, thou hast eaten so much liverwort that it is growing out of thy head;" to which he humbly replied, "Now it is your turn." And thus receiving mortification from many people, by God's grace he grew better and better, and persevered to the end.

CHAPTER XII

*Of the great Mortification Practised by the Blessed
Giovanni during a Journey to Montecchiello.*

IOVANNI, the servant of Christ, was once
going to Montecchiello with Francesco Vincenti, Vanni, and another of his companions, and
when they came near San Giovanni at Asso, and
were passing the estates which Giovanni had given
to the Convent of Santa Bonda, he, wishing to punish
himself for his sins in every place where he had
lived, stripped himself almost naked, and ordered his
companions to drag him by a cord through all the
villages of the district, beating him at the same time;
and he told the one who held the rope to say, "Look
at this fellow, who wanted to starve you, who every
year gave you old corn which had been spoilt by
the weevils, and then asked for the good new corn
more than was right, and wanted to charge it a
florin a bushel. Give it to him well, this cruel man,

4

who hates the poor." And in this way they led him through the villages, beating him, and dragging him by the cord so fiercely, that he could hardly breathe, and they obediently did and said all that he commanded them; and the people, astonished at this strange sad sight, and at his thus mortifying himself before them, their compassion and admiration were so great that not one of them was able to say a word. Afterwards the humble Giovanni said to his brothers, " Christ will reward you for your obedience and charity towards me, yet do not think that the sinful and unholy desires which I used to have in these places are atoned for ; rather I deserve to be dragged in this way over the whole country."

CHAPTER XIII

Of the Conversion of Messer Domenico of Montecchiello.

ANOTHER time when the man of God Giovanni was going to Montecchiello with his poor brothers, they stopped at Corsignano ; and there preaching Christ's Name, very great honour was shown towards them, and having rested there for the night, they left the next morning, though with great difficulty. But when they had gone a little way, the men of Corsignano sent after them, praying them for God's sake to return ; for one of their place said he had had a vision, in which he had seen men drowning, and they were saved from danger and from death by the hands of Giovanni and his companions : so these poor brothers in their charity returned to Corsignano, and there gained much fruit. After this, when they reached Montecchiello, they found many of the people there very hard and obstinate, and they had to bear a great deal of

4 *

suffering and ill-treatment from them for Christ's sake. And when Giovanni, the servant of God, noticed that the people neither feared God nor kept His commandments, he saw in the spirit the scourge that God had prepared for them. For more than twenty years before he had warned them that if they did not repent they should be destroyed, and so it happened ; for in the war that followed between the Siennese and Florentines, Montecchiello was ruined and plundered. However, I cannot say that the man of God Giovanni gained *no* fruit there, because Messer Domenico of Montecchiello, a doctor of laws, and Monna Antonia, his wife, were converted by his holy words. This Messer Domenico was one of his first companions; he devoted himself to God's service, and had very great spiritual knowledge; he was also a man of many tears and much prayer. He translated, for the comfort of Giovanni and his companions, a little book of Mystic Theology which had been written by a holy man, a Carthusian. The twelve nobles who governed the city at that time made Domenico the vicar for the year at Petriuolo, which office he held with Giovanni's consent, and afterwards, when Giovanni and his brothers went to Montecchiello, they usually stayed at his house.

Another man from this place, called Francesco, also followed the man of God Giovanni in the way of holy poverty, and when he was converted, he presented himself to his wife and children barefooted and poor, like his companions, and by his self-mortification and humiliation, his wife was converted also.

CHAPTER XIV.

What the Blessed Giovanni did in Montalcino.

AFTER this, Giovanni, the servant of God, and his poor brothers, went to Montalcino, and there preached about God, and the salvation of the soul, which excited such fervour of weeping and lamentation throughout the place, that many men and women heartily changed their lives; and amongst those who were converted to Christ were Fazio di Betto, who became one of Giovanni's followers, never to leave him again; also Agostino and his wife Binda. This man afterwards grew so very fervent, that whenever he heard Christ spoken of, he could not resist crying out in the excess of his fervour, and it was just the same with his wife. Another man, also, called Barna, became poor for Christ's sake: he was a devout servant of God, and sang many holy hymns. One Monna Jacopa of this place, who had a husband and four children, was also converted;

and of her Giovanni used to say that he had never seen any one more ardent or self-denying. She was very often so overcome by her fervour that she was almost beside herself, so that once she fell into the fire; and sometimes, when she was going along the road, she fell into the mud: she was a woman of many tears, and very humble and charitable.

Once, when Giovanni and his companions were at Montalcino, they were joined by Francesco di Montecchiello; and one Sunday evening, when Francesco was taking the discipline, in the oratory belonging to the Flagellants, with whom the poor ones of Christ were staying, such sudden fervour was kindled in his heart by Christ, that he hardly slept all that night, nor could Giovanni sleep either. Francesco declared that till that moment he had never known Christ, and that all his works hitherto had been dark and deceitful; and the next night his fervour was still greater, he shed many tears, and could not refrain from crying out and leaping for joy. This astonished Giovanni greatly, for Francesco had only lately become a follower of Christ, and he (Giovanni) had never said anything to him which could give rise to such strong feelings. When Francesco returned to Montecchiello, he went about the place, proclaiming the name of Christ with such earnestness that people thought he was mad.

Giovanni, the servant of God, remained some days in Montalcino, and while there, about twenty of his companions in poverty were taken ill with ague, which was a common complaint in those parts. Meo Martino of Montalcino was very kind to them, taking them sugar, wine, and other good things. Francesco di Montecchiello, his wife, and three old ladies also brought them plenty of provisions from Montecchiello. A young man, the nephew of Messer Cione, the Count of Montecchiello, came with Francesco, and before Giovanni and the others, he took off his shoes and stockings, and gave all his clothes and money to those ladies of Montecchiello, that they might give it to God; and so he became one of the poor of Jesus Christ. Francesco's wife and the other ladies were so greatly edified by the life and doctrine of Giovanni, the man of God, and his companions, that they returned to Montecchiello full of the love of Jesus Christ. Amongst those who were ill were Messer Domenico di Montecchiello, Ambrogio di Giucca, and Giovanni d'Ambrogio d'Agnolino, a citizen of Siena. This last would have died of his sickness, but owing to the prayers of Giovanni, the servant of God, and his companions, he was miraculously healed by God. During his illness, Giovanni said to him one day, " Tell me, Giovanni, which would you like best ? or which do you think I had better do? Give myself only to prayer, and wholly retire from the world, or go about preaching Christ ? " To this he replied, " Do not cease to preach Christ." And this was a cause of sorrow to himself till the day of his death, because he was of a weakly constitution.

They had been about fifteen days at Montalcino, when a young man who was on guard at the Castle there, entreated Giovanni so earnestly to receive him into his family, that he could not refuse his request ; and this youth suffered himself to be led through Montalcino, clad in his shirt only, with a halter round his neck, being abused and insulted at the same time. After this the humble Giovanni and his good brothers left Montalcino ; and they departed secretly, because of the great devotion in which they were held.

CHAPTER XV.

An Exhortation to Charity and Self-mortification.

IOVANNI, the man of God, said that he noticed throughout Christendom more virtuous acts than ever, more learning, more morality, more respect, more ceremonies, more offices; and that all would be holy, and *are* so in proportion as they contain charity, but of that he found scarcely any, at least, not the true sort which Christ kindles in the soul. And for this he only saw three remedies. First, to speak constantly of Jesus Christ, His love, and great benefits to the soul; for the more strongly a man speaks the more he feels. Secondly, to cultivate great love and charity for all creatures, to make much of them, and show them love without measure: he found that greater honour was done to Christ by this second rule than by a long sermon, for this kindles on both sides great feeling and fervour towards God. Thirdly, to mortify ourselves greatly, for

that takes us out of ourselves, and sets us free. If
these three rules, he said, were assiduously followed,
the soul would certainly gain by them: after that we
should wish to follow Christ in humility and gratitude.
In proof of this he related, that one day being in
Montecchiello, he there found three of his converts
wanting in fervour, so he enjoined them to mortify
themselves, and spoke joyfully to them of Christ.
They were immediately aroused to much thought of
God, and a child, the son of one of them, was suddenly seized with fervour, though he did not know
what it was. Fervour awoke also in the hearts of the
others, and they were so inflamed with Divine love
that they were willing to cast themselves into the
fire, or suffer any pain or shame for the honour of
Jesus Christ. For this reason the much-loving John
said to his dear brothers: "It is my opinion that virtues
are failing because we fail to speak enough of God,
for I have seen and known that, as a natural conse-
quence, the heart feels what the tongue utters; so he
whose talk is of the world, grows lukewarm and
worldly; he who speaks of Christ thinks of Christ.
Therefore, if you wish Christ to give Himself to you,
you will always be ready to speak, sing, or read of
Christ, or else to meditate on or pray to Him. You

must know that no worse temptation can befall a
man than that of hiding and being silent about the
blessings and gifts of God, because sweet converse
about Jesus Christ is food and life to the soul; and
Christ will never leave the soul who loves to talk of
Him. He will be always with him. Therefore, if
the whole world were to tell you not to speak of
Christ, you can laugh them to scorn; for whoever
will confess Him before men, him will He confess
before His Father. For this reason I exhort you never
to forget the holy art of speaking about God." Then
he cried out, vehemently, " Oh, let us not sleep; let
us proclaim the blessed Name of Christ by day and
night, in the streets and market-places: let us go to
hell, if need be, to proclaim It there and do It honour:
the *world* goes there because it does not remember It:
let *us* go there to proclaim and publish It: may the
most holy Name of Christ live for ever: let not
tongues be weary or hearts satiated with proclaiming Christ crucified: may He reign a thousand thousand years: may the most holy Name of Christ reign
for ever: may Christ reign over the world in the
hearts of all men. To Jesus Christ be all honour and
glory; to us shame and dishonour."

Once, when Giovanni, the servant of God, was in

Montecchiello, he went to see a sick man there; who, although he was very patient, groaned continually, and could take no rest, because his sickness was very painful. The compassionate John began to comfort him, exhorting him to continue patient to the end, telling him that God had laid that sickness on him for his good, and for his soul's health, and that he would be rewarded in the next world. After that, he wished to see him naked, and uncovered him, and seeing him full of sores, he felt great pity for him. Then, without the least dread or loathing, he bent over him tenderly, and for love of Christ licked him all over. That done, he said, "May the blessing of Christ be with thee, and be in peace, for God will help thee." As soon as John had left him he felt better, and was relieved of his pains. When John and his poor little ones were at dinner, great honour was done to them, and chickens were set before them; and the charitable Giovanni took one of them, and said to his companion, Vanni, "Take this, and carry it to that sick man, and bid him take comfort in Christ." Vanni immediately took it to him, and on seeing Vanni, the sick man was very glad, and said, "Tell Giovanni that, by God's mercy and by means of his charity, I am better, and my pains have left me."

Not long after that the sick man died, and for his constant patience under his great infirmities the gracious God worked miracles by him. Giovanni ate very little meat, and did not like it at all; but when it was set before him, not wishing to appear singular, he pretended to take some, as the others did. He used to sigh when he was at table, and often wept while eating.

CHAPTER XVI

What the Blessed Giovanni did at Asciano.

ANOTHER time, when Giovanni, the man of God, was walking with Francesco Vincenti and other companions towards the Castle of Asciano, they being hungry and weary, stopped at a poor countryman's door, and said to him, "For the love of God, we pray thee give us something to eat." The countryman replied, "I have but little, but of that little I will gladly give you." "Pray prepare us a little cabbage," they said. The countryman answered, "God knows that there is none here, for Anechino's troop of soldiers, and others besides, have cut away, not only leaves, but whole plants, and not a leaf is left in the neighbourhood." To this the servants of God replied, "Go and look about well, for perhaps thou mayest find some." And he said, "I will go, but I am sure there are not any." So he went, and found a quantity of beautiful cabbages, and wondering greatly,

he cut some and had them dressed. When the poor
of Jesus Christ were eating, they said again to the
countryman, "Canst thou give us a leek?" "Both
leeks and everything else that is eatable have been
plundered," he replied; "but if you wish, I will go
and see, and perhaps I might miraculously find some
leeks also;" and they told him to go. So he went,
and found some leeks, and brought them with great
joy, and every one wondered greatly at the cabbages
and the leeks, and they all thanked God, who works
wonders by His servants.

When the fervent Giovanni and his poor little ones
arrived at Asciano, they preached the Word of God
there; and the people of that place were moved to
such fervour that they blessed him who cried out,
"Glory to Christ crucified;" and they were so greatly
and miraculously inflamed with love, that it was a
marvellous sight to behold.   The above-mentioned
poor ones, and certain from Montalcino, who had
followed them, lodged with the Brothers Minor, who
entertained them most hospitably, and could not
make enough of them.   Amongst others of that place
who were converted to Christ was one Girolamo,
who became one of his most earnest companions.
He was a man of great intellect and great peni-

tence, of holy life and doctrine, and was often rapt in ecstasy.

Another time, when Giovanni, the man of God, was passing near Asciano, to avoid walking on the Sunday they remained in Asciano on Saturday (which is the festival* of our Lady) and the day following, and lodged at the house of James Messer Grifolo, who showed them much kindness. And there came Barna from Montecchiello, bringing him a letter from Francis. When the zealous John had read it, he left the house in great fervour of spirit, and he and the above-named Barna went about the place and neighbourhood, praising God with great gladness, so that the loving Giovanni said he then experienced sweeter sensations than he had ever before felt.

* La festività.

CHAPTER XVII.

An Exhortation to Holy Poverty by the Blessed Giovanni.

IOVANNI, the poor little one of Christ, said: "Give yourselves to Christ without measure, and despise everything else, for time is short, and we may not have long to stay here, and blessed are those who love Christ unsparingly. He who loves anything, except in God, that very thing prevents his loving God, and obscures his intellect; for just as anything we put over our bodily eyes hinders our seeing, so do the things we love out of God destroy our union with Him, and shut out the light of the truth of Jesus Christ. Holy poverty empties the soul of earthly cares and affections, and of all created things; and the soul thus lightened, when touched by God, is easily turned to contemplation of Him, and meditation on the Holy Passion of Jesus Christ. It feeds on, and takes pleasure in these things, lamenting

the time formerly misspent, and offences committed
against God, and is anxious by penance to take
vengeance on itself in every possible way; desiring
to be humble and patient, and very charitable towards all creatures, for the love of God; hating and
despising itself, and being ready to suffer insult, tor-
ment, or persecution, knowing God's goodness and
its own vileness and misery. Know, my brothers,
that Jesus Christ wishes you to be zealous lovers of
holy poverty, and to embrace it heartily; to avoid,
as you would poison, appropriating anything to
yourselves, for the devil will try to make you say, even
of a little thing, "This is mine." Do not be too
burdensome to people, for that is neither pleasing to
God or them; and keep holy poverty clean and pure,
not spoiling or corrupting it, for it is the foundation
on which all virtues are built, and the nurse of
humility; therefore, as we have no merit of our
own, but the merit of holy poverty, we have no desire
for the state or riches of the Emperor. "Poverty!
poverty!" he cried out, fervently, "thy language is
not understood. May holy poverty live in our
hearts!"

CHAPTER XVIII.

Of two Miracles which befell the Blessed Giovanni.

ONE day, when Giovanni and Francesco were tra-
velling with their poor brothers, on reaching
Torraniere, one of the company fell sick, so that he
could not eat. Then Giovanni went to him, and tried
to comfort him, asking him if he had an appetite for
anything in particular. "I fancy nothing," said the
sick man, "but a little lettuce salad : if I had that,
I think I should be cured." Upon this, the charitable
Giovanni went into the garden and looked about carefully for lettuces, but could not find any, and not
knowing what to do, for the sick man's longing was
great, he had recourse to Divine aid; and kneeling
down in the garden, he prayed God to provide for the
comfort of his poor one. When he had finished his
prayer, he saw before him a beautiful lettuce, and
taking it, he returned thanks, and joyfully bore it to
the invalid, who on eating it with an appetite was
quickly healed of his sickness.

Another time, when Giovanni, the lover of Christ, was walking with his devout brothers, they came to a large meadow, which was very full of flowers. His companions, being seized with sudden fervour of spirit, took hold of Giovanni, laid him on the ground, and very soon covered him with so many flowers, that he was completely hidden from view. After he had been a little while in that position they began to uncover him, and on removing the flowers from his face, it appeared so glorious and shining, that they could hardly bear the sight, and by degrees the splendour faded away.

CHAPTER XIX.

An Exhortation to Patience by the Blessed Giovanni.

THE fervent Giovanni said: " Let us rekindle our love in the burning charity of Jesus Christ; let us fully believe that as yet we have done no good thing, and bravely and earnestly begin again, waking up as the plants do, and preparing to bring forth much and holy fruit ; and with all humility, and for love of Christ, let us be patient with all men and under all adversities. God sends consolations and afflictions to the soul, that it may be benefited in all ways, just as the wise man is as glad of the frost in January as of the heat in May, knowing that the corn takes root beneath the ice. Therefore, do not be frightened at temptations, which are the life and crown of the soul : rather let us look for them cheerfully, and bear them bravely. Gold is refined and perfected in the fire, so let us rejoice at every tribulation, suffering, or temptation."

In fervour of spirit he said: "He who refuses to fight is already beaten; he who fights bravely is almost conqueror: therefore let us take up arms, and fight boldly for the Cross of Christ, always invoking His aid."

Once when John, the servant of God, had gone to Colombajo with his poor brothers, to visit that devout place, and the Brothers Minor there, it happened that a leaden pipe fell upon the head of his dear companion Giovanni d'Ambrogio, and he lost about ten pounds of blood. It was next to impossible that his natural strength should survive such a blow, but by the intercession of John, the man of God, he was miraculously healed.

Again, when the charitable Giovanni was at Siena, he heard that his friend and neighbour, Ludovico di Noddo of the Malescotti, was very ill, and at death's door, so he went to visit him. On his arrival he began to comfort him, beseeching him to have hope in Jesus Christ, and put his trust in God for help. "But what hope can I have?" said Ludovico: "you see that I am dying, I cannot live, and even now can hardly speak."

Giovanni answered him compassionately, and said, "Believe me, thou shalt recover, and not die of this sickness; and I tell thee further, thou shalt yet have a son." Ludovico could not believe it, but it happened as Giovanni had foretold, for he was cured of his sickness, and he afterwards had a son, to whom he gave the name of Agnolo.

The humble Giovanni said to his beloved brothers: "The Holy Gospel says if the grain of wheat does not die in the ground, it will not bear fruit. So must we die to the world, if we wish to bear fruit to God. Let us then forsake the world: you know Christ did not pray for the world, because it hated Him. Therefore if we wish Christ to love us, let us hate the world, with all its honours and everything belonging to it. Let us partake of the shame of Jesus Christ, and desire death with Him, being willing to shed our blood for Him, as He did for us." In fervour of spirit, he said: "I recommend Christ to you, who is neglected a thousand times more than you think. Christ is so neglected that the way of perfection and virtue is looked upon as a dream; and it seems to me that he who loves Christ ought to dress in sad colours, weep, and die of grief. Let him therefore who loves Christ mourn and weep, for even a felon would not be treated as our Lord Jesus Christ is treated: therefore, my Lord being so neglected, I would willingly die to everything, if by any pain or poverty I could recover His lost honour. It is such pain and grief to me not to hear the Blessed Christ spoken of as He should be, that I can hardly contain myself, and am ready to die; and if you knew what I know by experience, you would never cease to love Him, or to speak of Him by day and night. Pray to God for me that my wish may be granted; namely, that I may see and hear this loudly proclaimed all over the world, 'All Glory to Christ Crucified!' and then may God do what He wills with me.

CHAPTER XX.

How, owing to the Malice of some, they were Banished from Siena.

OW as the said servants of God were increasing in number and merit, and growing in grace and virtue before God and man, the enemy of mankind, being envious at seeing so many souls enter the way of salvation, made use of the tongues of certain murmurers, who wickedly persuaded the twelve lords of Siena then in power, that Giovanni Colombini and Francesco Vincenti, the leaders of the poor ones of Jesus Christ, should be banished beyond their territory, fearing the injury and depopulation of the city from the multitude of people who left the world (which they thought they were chiefly bound to serve). So Giovanni and Francesco were commanded under pain of death to leave the city before a little lighted candle, which was carried to the gate, should be burnt out. Joyfully did the servants of God receive this sentence

of banishment, knowing, as the Apostle said, that
here they had no abiding city, but they sought that
one eternal in the heavens, from which they could
not be banished, unless they frowardly rebelled
against Christ; and so, rejoicing at their persecution
for righteousness' sake, and singing and shouting for
joy, they left Siena and went to Arezzo. But no
sooner were they gone, than the sky grew dark, and
there came a heavy thunderstorm, and with it such
rain and hail, that people thought it was the end of the
world. At the same time also a great many of the
Siennese were stricken with fever. Upon this miraculous wonder, the twelve lords released Giovanni
and Francesco from their banishment, and restored
them to their former position, sending to ask their
pardon, and praying them to return to Siena.

CHAPTER XXI.

What the Blessed Giovanni did at Arezzo.

OW the servants of God, Giovanni and Francesco, with twenty-five of their companions, having arrived at Arezzo, and entering the city singing and praising Jesus Christ, all the country was moved to see and hear them; and preaching there the Word of God, they gained great fruit there, so that hundreds of sinners, who had lived many years without confession, repented of their sins, and confessed themselves. By the admonition of these servants of God, many who had been robbed of their good name, or their possessions, obtained restitution, many enmities were extinguished, and some deadly quarrels appeased, and these men were universally held in great reverence and esteem. Not only the citizens, but many people from the surrounding country, came to listen to the salutary exhortations and good advice of these poor for Jesus Christ.

At that time Vanni of Montecchiello fell sick at the monastery of Santa Bonda, where the said poor ones resided; and perceiving his sickness was increasing, he was very anxious to see Giovanni, his father in Christ, before he died: and he so urgently entreated his poor companions, that, moved by charity, they bore him to Arezzo in a litter. They entered the city by night (for the gates were left open, owing to the multitude of country people who were coming or going), and in the suburbs and the streets they met a great many people with lights in their hands, who were returning from hearing Giovanni preach. On inquiring for him, they were told that he lodged with a company of secular Flagellants, but it would be almost impossible to speak to him, because of the number of people who were about him. Nevertheless, they went to the said fraternity, and spoke to some of the brothers, saying, " We have brought Vanni here, who is ill, and wishes to see Giovanni, our father." They replied, " It would be impossible at present, but let us put him in the room where Giovanni sleeps, so that at least, when he goes to bed, he may see him, and we will do our best to inform him of the matter; " and so they did. But when the charitable Giovanni heard that

his friend Vanni, whom he greatly loved, was lying
there ill, he said, "Tell him to wait patiently, while
I send away this company;" and having very gently
ordered every one to return home, he said, "Where
is my Vanni?" and they led him to him. When
Giovanni, the man of God, saw him lying on the bed,
he began to comfort him with very soothing words,
and, constrained by charity, he took off his cloak and
laid it upon Vanni, who, as soon as the cloak touched
him, felt quite well; and, entirely cured of his sickness, he rose from the bed, and he and his companions heartily thanked God for the new blessing
of this miraculous cure.

CHAPTER XXII.

An Exhortation to Humility by the Blessed Giovanni.

THE humble Giovanni said to his beloved brothers: "God has sown in us the seed of good works, and therefore if this seed should spring up, increase and multiply, we must not glory in it, for it is not our own, and we cannot bear any fruit of ourselves; but let us glory in Jesus Christ, who is our true glory. The better the seed that is sown in us, and the better fruit we bear, so much the more do we owe to the Sower—that is, God; and the more we increase in good works, the greater is our obligation to the good and gracious God, because by ourselves we can do nothing. Therefore, if any virtue grows in us, that of humility ought to increase above all, for the more grace we have, the more will be expected of us. Great is our debt, and quite* unable are we to pay it. We must be careful to call ourselves only unprofitable servants; and so indeed

* Poverissimi.

we are, for it is only by grace that we receive grace. We have good cause for weeping, and for thinking whether even the soldiers may not rise in judgment against us; and I doubt not that if God had given them half the help He has to us, they would have done far more than we have. Alas! I am full of fear, and I think rightly so; for if the receiving of heavenly gifts entitled one to eternal life, who ever deserved it more than Solomon? God was so pleased by his praying for wisdom, that He gave more to him than to any other man in the world. He built His holy temple, and was endued with great wisdom, so that he was enabled to perceive that everything belonging to the world was "vanity of vanities;" and yet, notwithstanding all this, S. Augustine believes that he is damned. Also, how many there have been who had great spiritual knowledge, some who have been gifted with learning, some with prophecy, some with working of miracles, and they are now in hell! because in virtue only, and in doing the will of God, lies our happiness and our safety. He is not God's friend who only thinks of Him, but he who follows up that thought by virtuous living; because to whom Christ gives much, of him will He ask the more: therefore, the servant who knows his Lord's will, and does it not, shall be beaten with many stripes. For these reasons, I think that pride, not thanking God for His blessings, and not being in charity with all men, destroys every other good gift we may possess.

CHAPTER XXIII.

What the Blessed Giovanni did in the City of Castello.

AFTER spending some days in Arezzo, and gaining much fruit there, the Blessed Giovanni and his poor companions departed, and went towards the city of Castello. And when they were near it, they saw a peasant, called Santi, ploughing his field, to whom Giovanni, the man of God, called with a loud voice, telling him to follow Christ; upon which he left the oxen and the plough, and went with Giovanni, and never returned to his husbandry. He was a very charitable, holy man, and often had beautiful visions of angels. Entering Castello, the Blessed Giovanni and his fervent brothers went first to the principal church, as their custom was, and on their way, in the street of the Tartarini, they met Benedetto di Pace, the Bishop's notary, and Giovanni looking on him, and being assured by the Spirit of his salvation, said to him suddenly, " Come with me, thou ill-living old man ; leave the world, and follow Christ." Benedetto (the grace of God converting him) immediately accompanied Giovanni, and afterwards became one of his poor brothers. After saying their prayers in the Duomo, they went about the place, praising Jesus Christ, and exhorting all persons to turn to God, and be converted; so that the whole city was moved to exclaim, "Praised be Jesus Christ, blessed be the Name of Christ." And very many men and women, seeing the fervour of the Blessed Giovanni and his companions, and hearing their holy exhortations, were converted, and became true penitents. Amongst others who forsook the world, and joined the poor ones of Jesus Christ, was one called Stefano, a man of rare intellect, who became a devoted servant of God; and another called Bartoluccio di Santi, who was so inflamed with Divine love, that whenever he heard any one speaking earnestly of God, he could not remain quiet. To mention one instance. One day, when he was listening with other citizens to a sermon in the Church of San Fiordo in that city, such fervour was kindled in him that he could no longer contain the ardour of his spirit: he ran out of the church, and leapt into the square, without touching any of the church steps. Many times against his will he made the bystanders laugh with astonishment. The said Bartoluccio, Giovanni di Jacopo, and another of the principal inhabitants of the place, called Ghingo, showed much kindness to the poor brothers.

They were also favourably received by Messer Buccio, the Bishop of that city, a very kind-hearted man ; and he grew so fond of the Blessed Giovanni and his companions, that he was on the most friendly and intimate terms with them ; and he thought that to be a member of their company was better than even the pontifical dignity; so he joined them, and they regarded him as their beloved father. The Blessed Giovanni, perceiving that Messer Buccio was most strictly conscientious, and learned in canonical law, and remembering that Domenico di Montecchiello had advised them, for the better security of their congregation, to obtain Apostolic sanction, asked the said Bishop if what they were doing was contrary to any decree, or could be deemed suspicious in any way, and if he thought they ought to apply to the Cardinal, who was then the Legate at Viterbo, for a license. He replied that they did nothing which was against rule, or could be thought so, therefore he did not think it necessary for them to ask for sanction : they were poor, simple, and pure-minded men, with no earthly cares, and so they might safely leave all in God's hands. These words of His good vicar, the

Canonist, comforted them greatly, and the Blessed Giovanni was much pleased by them; and as the said Bishop was of holy life and doctrine, these poor ones always asked his advice on all important matters, and to his death he continued their zealous and loving friend; and not he alone, but all the bishops of that province were their great benefactors and protectors. The charity of these soldiers of Jesus Christ was so great, that finding a great sinner in the city who would not repent, the Blessed Giovanni, being very anxious for his salvation, said to him, "If thou wilt forsake thy sins, I will give thee all my merits, and every good thing I have ever done;" and the ardent Francesco said to him, "And *I* will gladly take all the sins thou hast committed on myself, if thou wilt truly turn to God;" each of them making him these offers from his heart. And this sinner (the grace of God and their good counsel aiding him) became a true penitent.

I must not omit to mention three beneficial works which were done by these poor for Jesus' sake, early in Lent, before they left that place. First, they accepted and received two men into their company. One was Perugino, who had been a bad man, the other was a secular priest: he had been a proud and wicked man, but he gave up a good benefice and did much penance. Second, the before-named Benedetto di Pace, much to the satisfaction of the Blessed Giovanni and his companions, placed his niece with the sisters of the convent Del Sacco. Up to that time these sisters had each kept her own possessions to herself, but from that day, by the grace of God and the good advice of the poor ones of Jesus Christ, six of the richest of them began to live in common, refusing to call anything their own. The third thing worthy of remembrance was that, owing to the gentle and peaceful words of the merciful Giovanni and his brothers, a citizen of Siena, of the noble house of Tolomei, called Larino, who, out of devotion to the Blessed Giovanni, had accompanied him from Arezzo to Castello, did, in the presence of the above-named Bishop, make peace with, and fully pardon, three of the family of the Piccoluomini, for the murder of his uncle, Meo di Larino Tolomeo. A thousand florins could not have bought this peace. The charitable Giovanni sent the public announcement of it to Siena, with a loving and tender epistle to these three Piccoluomini, and by this action he not only made peace between these two families, but brought about their friendship.

CHAPTER XXIV.

An Exhortation to Holy Living by the Blessed Giovanni.

ITH great fervour Giovanni said to his brothers: "Let us, dearly beloved, mourn and weep, and take bitter vengeance on ourselves; for if we were guilty of no other sin but that of ingratitude, and of despising and almost refusing God (who, whether we will or no, gives Himself to us, while we, proud, ungrateful wretches that we are, wanting in faith and ardour, receive this immeasurable gift with irreverence and coldness, and keep it carelessly), we ought to seek to die for Him a thousand times, if such were possible. We ought, all of us, to be lion-hearted, ready to endure anything for the love of Christ crucified, and if this were our will, other things would be of little importance. It is our duty to exercise ourselves in holy desire and fervent prayer, even with a loud voice; and in all holy virtues, especially in perfect love to God and our neighbour, and holy humility. Therefore, my dear brethren, since the Lord has called and chosen us to a higher degree of perfection, we are bound to do everything as perfectly as possible, that we may not be reproached as liars or deceivers: but, above all, let us act so that our light may shine, and give forth bright rays, that our Heavenly Father may be honoured in us, and that by our good example, many, forsaking their sins, may return into the way of truth, together with us honouring our Lord Jesus Christ: and doing this with purity and charity, we shall live happily and in the joy of the Holy Ghost, and continue in this to a happy death, which will lead us to true and everlasting life."

These poor ones of Jesus Christ went to a village on the mountain of Siena, called Arcidosso, where they gained much fruit. Among those of that place who were converted to God, was one called Giusto, who became an ardent follower of Giovanni, the man of God, in the way of holy poverty. He led a very strict life, and always slept on the bare ground or on a plank.

And thus these servants of God went about the cities and villages, preaching the Name of Jesus

Christ. Not once only did they visit the places mentioned, but they often returned, both to encourage their companions who lived there (for they did not all preach) in the service of God, and also to exhort sinners again to repentance. They most frequently lodged with the secular Flagellants, because these confraternities of the discipline showed them much kindness.

CHAPTER XXV.

Of some Miracles worked by the Blessed Giovanni.

ONCE, when Giovanni, the servant of Christ, was at Montalcino, he thought of his first companion, Francesco Vincenti, who was then at Siena, and who now never cut his hair or his nails, or shaved his beard, so that he looked like a wild man; and the Blessed Giovanni thinking this a useless penance, he was allowed, by God's will, to appear to Francesco in a dream, telling him that severity to the body was pleasing to God, but not too great austerity of life, and that this singularity was very dangerous; and on waking in the morning, and considering his dream, Francesco immediately shaved his beard, and cut his hair and nails. After this, Giovanni, the man of God, wrote to Siena, saying: "Tell Francesco that he has done well to obey;"

at which he was much astonished, for he had not told any one of the vision.

Nor can I by any means keep silence about a wonderful miracle worked by our Lord Jesus Christ, to show the holy doctrine and life of His most devoted servant, Giovanni; which is, that once, while the Blessed Giovanni and some of his poor companions were talking earnestly, round a great fire, about the edification of souls, one of them, being tempted by the devil, contradicted, and spoke rudely; so Giovanni, the man of God, commanded him to be silent, and ordered him by holy obedience to put his head under the burning logs which were on the hearth. He, being sorry for his presumptuous words, implicitly obeying his holy father, laid his head directly under the burning wood, and kept it there till Giovanni, the servant of God, gave him leave to remove it. What I shall relate is very wonderful, but yet true. When this poor obedient man stood up, not only was his head not burnt, but not a single hair was injured; and all the bystanders, astonished at such a grand miracle, and perceiving the sanctity of their master and father, never dared afterwards to contradict him in the least thing. Amongst those present was the before-mentioned Vanni of Montecchiello, who survived Giovanni, the man of God, more than forty years, and who often related this miracle with great devotion, and also the gift of holiness which he received at Arezzo, by virtue of the power of the Blessed Giovanni.

CHAPTER XXVI.

A Discourse on Humility by the Blessed Giovanni.

THE humble Giovanni said: "The Blessed Jesus Christ is the only one who can set us free from the many and great struggles which we all have to maintain in our journey through this short life. They are so frequent, that our strength would utterly fail if it were not for the pitying help of our merciful and tender Father; and this we need, not only on rare occasions, and in great dangers, but hourly, and on the least occasion. And we require to be not only helped, but almost forcibly held and borne up, for if the good God let go His Hand from us, we should soon fall into every sort of wretchedness. Therefore, if we see that without His continual support we cannot stand upright, but fallin to great sin, what shall we say of any virtue that we practise, be it one or many, great or small? Should we wish, or ought we to glory in ourselves, as if our virtue was our own? Let us not on this score become proud or presumptuous, despising others and exalting ourselves. I think we should be worthy of double condemnation, if, while receiving great blessings and gifts from God and Jesus Christ, we should become less holy, or fail in the virtue of humility: hence, the upright proud man is more displeasing to Him than the humble sinner. Therefore, my dear brethren, the more we have of Divine light and grace, the more clearly shall we perceive our misery and frailty, for we shall see that our actions fall far short of our duty. In short, the more we by God's grace draw nigh to Him with holy virtues, so much the more shall we be illuminated, and the better we shall know that He is the Author of all goodness and strength, and we are utterly vile and weak."

CHAPTER XXVII

Of what more befell the Blessed Giovanni at Arezzo.

ANOTHER time, when the very ardent Giovanni returned to Arezzo with some of his poor ones, they passed the night in a hospital belonging to the Eremitani brothers, the governor of which was a very good man, who showed much hospitality to pilgrims, especially to religious. When the hour of rest came, the Blessed Giovanni, being fatigued in body and mind, unfastened the coat that covered his chest, in order to lie down on one of the beds. As soon as it was opened, such a brilliant light shone from that holy breast, that the hospital at night was as light as at noon-day, and the brightness was so great, that the bystanders could not in any way bear to look upon that holy breast.

Once Giovanni, the charitable, and some of his poor brothers, were spending the evening of the Carnival in the same house, and cold meat soaked in vinegar

was provided for their supper; upon which one of the
poor brothers, moved by his love for the Blessed
Giovanni, said, "There is one here who has a weak
stomach, and much vinegar is hurtful to him."
When they were all at table, before they began to eat,
Giovanni, the man of God, being kindled by Divine
fire, began to speak earnestly of the love of God, and
how Divine love warms not the soul only, but sometimes the body also; and he grew so animated in his
talk, that they spent the whole night in these holy
discourses. When these poor ones of Jesus Christ
saw that the morning was come, without having had
any supper, they went to church, to cast ashes on
their heads.

CHAPTER XXVIII.

*An Exhortation on Loving God and our Neighbour by
the Blessed Giovanni.*

IOVANNI, inspired with love, said: "Let us,
my beloved brethren, renew holy ardour and
desire in ourselves; and although we are much to be
blamed for the time we have lost, let us not be too
much occupied with that thought, lest we should fall
into despair; but rather let us go confidently to our
good Jesus, and ask, like one who did so formerly,
which are the commandments most pleasing to Him;
and He will answer and say to us, 'Love me above
all things, with all your heart, with all your strength,
with all the powers of your mind and body;' and then,
'For the love I bear to you, love your neighbour as
yourselves.' These words, so sweet and dear, you
must know are part of life eternal, and the witness of
them in ourselves is the love and charity we bear towards each other. Who then can say that he loves

7

his neighbour far off, if he does not love his brother at his side? And if thou sayest, 'He has faults,' consider in thyself whether thou hast not as many: if thou lookest carefully, thou shalt find much greater in thyself. Therefore, my dear brethren, love each other with love kindled by the fire of the Holy Spirit; speak, each of you, that which will give glory to God and spiritual consolation to your fathers and brothers; let the elder reprove and correct the younger compassionately, and with paternal love, and the younger meekly take whatever chastisement is given to them. Also be more tender and respectful, one with the other, and strive to pray to God more for each other; so you will all be holy, wise, and kind, and your lives will be full of happiness. Rejoice in God, that He may rejoice in you. The time for our work is very short, and the reward is beyond all measure; and even if our life were long, still it is better to live in the joy of holiness than in the remorse and pain which are caused by sin."

CHAPTER XXIX.

How the Blessed Giovanni Established a Convent for Women.

ON the return of the Blessed Giovanni to Siena, he felt more and more strongly that a life of entire poverty was the most sure way of salvation, so he tried to establish this most salutary rule amongst women also. And thinking that a relation of his, called Caterina, daughter of Tommaso Colombini, his father Pietro's brother, was a fit person to begin such an order, because she was of good understanding, he tried as much as possible to persuade her to choose this life; and so he often talked to her about the edification of the soul and the great treasures of virtue, and especially of the merits and blessings of deep poverty. But she could not bear to hear the name of poverty, still less would she consent to accept such a rule of life, for she was rich, and delicately brought up. Yet she was a virgin, and did

7 *

not wish to marry. Giovanni, the man of God, was not a little grieved at this, and he often prayed to Jesus Christ, that He would be pleased so to touch her heart as to incline her to holy poverty. And so it pleased God to do ; for Giovanni, the charitable, being one evening at home with his wife, he called Caterina, who lived close to them, to a window which overlooked their house, and asked her what she was doing, and whether she was going to say her prayers ; and she replied, " To say the truth, I am just going to bed, and you see that the lamp in my hand is just refilled for that purpose." And Giovanni, in his ardour, again began exhorting her to renounce the world entirely, with all its false pleasures, and to become a lover of Jesus Christ and His holy virtues, especially that of holy poverty; showing her by many arguments, authorities, and examples, that whoever trusts in God, and with all his heart places his hope in Him, is never forsaken in his need; that as even the birds of the air are cared for by Jesus Christ, much more so are the creatures He has redeemed by His precious Blood. Amongst other examples, he told her of the widow in the time of Elisha the prophet, whose pot of oil was multiplied by God ; and he added, " In the same way, God can cause this light

not to go out, as He has already done to many saints."
Caterina listened most attentively to these burning
words, which, Giovanni perceiving, he continued the
whole night talking with her of the very great blessings of holy poverty, and of the many virtues and
graces which are gained by it. But God having
already begun to soften her heart, she did not perceive
that the night was passing away, and the morning
dawned upon this holy conversation.   When the
Blessed Giovanni saw that the sun had risen, he said
to her, "Go and lie down;" and she, turning to depart, perceived that daylight was entering by the win-
dows, and said with the greatest astonishment, "It is
broad daylight!"   But Giovanni, the servant of God,
replied, "How can it be daylight?   See your lamp, it
is still full."   And looking at the light which she had
held in her hand all the time, and seeing that it had
not grown dim, she understood that the merciful God
had worked a miracle in proof of the wholesome
words of the Blessed Giovanni; and being converted
by the will of Jesus Christ, and the assurance of this
miracle, she said to Giovanni, the man of God, "My
father, from this hour do what you will, for I am resolved, by God's help, to do all to His honour."   And
together with some ladies who had also been persuaded

by the holy words of the Blessed Giovanni to devote
themselves to Jesus Christ, she began to dress as a
poor person, and to beg her bread, for the love of God.
And so proceeding in the love of holy poverty and
other virtues, by her holy life and doctrine she helped
to turn women to repentance; following her friend
and father Giovanni, with some other ladies, in the
company and under the care of the older poor ones
of Jesus Christ. Amongst others of that place who
were converted to Christ, and became companions of
the devout Caterina, was a young woman called
Giovanna, daughter of Francesco dei Malescotti, and
another called Petra, daughter of one named Petro,
who was himself afterwards a brother of the magnificent hospital in that town. Also Francesca d'Ambrogio
d'Agnolo, sister of Giovanni d'Ambrògio, who has
been so often mentioned in these pages, and Andrea,
who was one of the first to begin this life in Florence.
They were also joined by Simona, daughter of Ristoro
of Fazio di Gallerani, who, after the death of those
above named, was left head and guide to all the
others. Her heart was on fire with charity, and by
her holy example and her wholesome words she drew
many into their poor company. They all gave themselves to mental prayer, holy reading, and useful

occupations, working with their own hands; and what they wanted for their support they begged, for the love of God.   They went barefoot, clad in coarse undyed cloth, their heads covered with a piece of linen ; and when the younger ones went out seeking alms, they were always accompanied by one of the elder sisters : they walked with downcast eyes, and were never out long at one time.   Thus they all lived together at first in Caterina's house.

CHAPTER XXX.

Exhortations to love Christ.

Addressed to the Sisters of his Company by the Blessed Giovanni.

GIOVANNI, the charitable, said to the ardent Caterina, and the sisters belonging to the company of poor ones of Jesus Christ: "Dearest sisters, my desire is that Christ may be glorified, and that each one of you may be His holy, true, and faithful spouse and handmaiden, a temple and tabernacle where He may rest. Prepare for Him a furnished chamber, that is, a pure heart, adorned with virtues, and the unruffled bed of holy love. Learn how to love, dear sisters, and feed on love. She who loves not Jesus Christ is not alive, but dead, for love is the true life of the soul: the soul which loves fears nothing, but that which loves not is very sad and desponding of her salvation. Remember, my beloved, if you would be heirs of Christ, keep His commandment of love, which was the Testament He left us. He did not lay many burdens upon us, but one only, and that is love. He who has love has Christ Himself, who is the fire of love, and possessing Him, he possesses all virtues. No one can really love his neighbour if he is not filled with the true love of God and Christ. The direct way of approaching Him is by holy contemplation, which can only be reached by the ladder of love. Love begets love, and it is attained by ardent and holy desire. Flee then to the mount of holy contemplation, on which is a lofty rock, where you need fear no enemies; not even the strongest can come there, where all is light, not darkness: on that rock is safety without fear. Retire to the recesses of your own consciences, and close the door against evil thoughts, which are like fierce and savage beasts; then enter into the caverns and secret places of pure and holy desires, and meditate on the great God, and His only-begotten Son, His holy Passion, His great and excellent gifts, and those unspeakable blessings, the mere recollection of which overpowers the soul with love. Therefore, my beloved mothers, sisters, and daughters in Christ, rouse yourselves to holy and zealous deeds and words; be, all of you, satiated, burning, and radiant with love; love each other with perfect charity, flee from sin, and from every person or thing which may turn you from holy love, but seek and make use of every person or thing which may help you to it. Be also wise and prudent, and do not suffer yourselves to take offence at anything, but be patient under every trial, for patience is the best evidence of your love to Christ.

"How many saints have been glad to be accounted fools for the sake of this love : how many have cheerfully waited for death under every form of suffering. Let your whole hearts be set on seeking Jesus Christ, and I must tell you you will not find Him by going from church to church, or by wandering about the world, but by continuing steadfast in prayer, holy conversation, and good thoughts. Let each, as a loving spouse of Jesus Christ, give her dear Husband and Lord the honour due unto Him. If an earthly wife obeys, honours, and strives to please her husband, how much more should the wife of the Heavenly Spouse? Do not seek to obey or love Him a little, but rather try how much honour and worship you can offer to Him. Jesus Christ, your Spouse, wishes for two especial honours from you: first, that you should be humble and full of charity; second, that forsaking all worldly affections, and being loosened from every earthly tie, you should often in contemplation fly heavenwards, and there feed, still keeping His holy Passion in remembrance, for that is the right gate and direct road to the vision of God. If you persevere in the love of Jesus Christ, and the practice of virtue, everything that you devoutly ask of your Spouse will be granted to you, according to His promise to those who ask in faith."

CHAPTER XXXI.

*What the Blessed Giovanni did for the Convent of
Santa Bonda.*

HEN the Blessed Giovanni by his holy exhortations, added to the wisdom and discretion of
Donna Paula, daughter of Ghino Foresi, Abbess of the
above-mentioned Convent of Santa Bonda, had induced all the nuns to live in common, they having at
first retained their own property, he persuaded many
citizens of Siena to place their daughters there, and
advised many young women to maintain holy virginity,
and become the spouses of Jesus Christ; and many
in the convent, especially his own relations, became
nuns, owing to his persuasive words. One Palm
Sunday five girls of noble birth were taken there by
the ardent Giovanni, bearing olive garlands on their
heads, and branches of olive in their hands. The
daughter of Francesco Vincenti, whose name was
Giovanna, when she became a nun was called Sister

Francesca.   In the thirteenth year of her age, having been professed in the order, her spirit returned to God. Agnola, the daughter of the Blessed Giovanni, received in the convent the name of Sister Maddalena, in honour of S. Mary Magdalene, for whom the loving Giovanni had an especial devotion ; and within a year after she entered the convent she also went to God.

When the very devout Giovanni lived in Siena, he often visited the Convent of Santa Bonda, not only for the purpose of exhorting the nuns to persevere in God's holy service, but also for the sake of the consolation he derived from the odour of their very great virtues, for the great God endued them with so much light and grace, that they were esteemed the holiest nuns in all Italy; so much so, that the Blessed Giovanni affirmed that Christ and a multitude of angels lived in the convent; and many signs of this were given, of which I will only relate one.   One night, when Ambrogio, one of Giovanni's companions, was near the place, at the house where they lodged strangers, he distinctly heard a host of demons leave the convent, with much noise and lamentation, like an army discomfited and routed; and this defeat, the Blessed Giovanni said, was a sign that Christ abode amongst them, on account of the virtues, especially

the great love and charity, which they possessed.
Giovanni, the man of God, was so impressed by the
sanctity of the Abbess and the other nuns, that when
he went to visit them, he often shed tears of devotion
the whole way from the gate of the city to the convent. And once, when he was talking to the Abbess
at the gate, of the most holy charity and sweet love
of Jesus Christ, and the unspeakable gifts and graces
which He grants to all who serve Him faithfully, they
were so inflamed by this Divine converse, that,
without being aware of it, they spent the whole
night in that employment. The Blessed Giovanni
had such faith and trust in this venerable and holy
Abbess, and loved and revered her so much, that he
obeyed her in everything, as he would a spiritual
Father, and wished all his poor companions to do
the same.

CHAPTER XXXII

An Exhortation to Patience by the Blessed Giovanni.

THE Blessed Giovanni said to his much-loved nuns of Santa Bonda : " Dearest mothers and sisters in Jesus Christ, let us purge out the old leaven, that we may be a new paste ; let us humble ourselves before Christ, turning to Him in ardour and charity, with consciences purged from sin ; let us break the chains which bind us fast, and hold us back from Christ ; and in self-abandonment let us de- vote ourselves to Him, Who, for us miserable sinners, willingly suffered such great and undeserved pains. In God's Name let us open our eyes and bewail our misspent time : till now we have only been intent on receiving good ; henceforth let us think a little what return we can make. We must be no longer weak children, but strong men, able to bear any wind which blows, not troubled or turned from Christ by any adversity."

In fervour of spirit he added : " Oh ! if we loved

our true Friend, Jesus Christ, we should for very fealty be willing to die for Him. Oh! let us die for Him who died for us. There is no greater proof of love than to be ready to die for a friend. If our love was perfect, we should be more grieved at offending God than at our own damnation,* because we ought to love Him better than ourselves. How much then should we love those who afflict us! kiss the hands which strike us! bless the tongue which curses us! love him who persecutes us! One only should we hate—ourselves—as the worst friend we have. Remember what that devout servant of God, S. Francis, said, that 'we ought greatly to love those who persecute us, because they help us to conquer our enemy, and beat down our tyrant, *i. e.*, ourselves, and our own concupiscence.' Oh, wretched man that I am! I leave the straight and shortest way, to wander in crooked and tedious paths. What avails it, our talking or knowing much about God and holiness, if we refuse the way that leads to it, and will not walk therein? This thought does not allow me to speak or write with a clear conscience, for the good opinion of others will not make me, such a sinner as I am, the less displeasing to God. Oh, what

* Compare the prayer of St. Gertrude before Communion.

shall I do ? I shall certainly die if I do not enter on this way of holiness. I ask you, therefore, dear spouses and sisters of Jesus Christ, to aid me by your holy prayers, beseeching God to help me to love Him in purity and truth, that not only I may hate myself, but that others may hate me also, that so I may make some little return for His great love towards me."

CHAPTER XXXIII.

*What the Blessed Giovanni did in the Convent of the
Preaching Friars at Siena.*

THERE came once some ambassadors from
Pisa to Siena, who, hearing of this newly-
formed society, wished to show their devotion to its
holy founders, the servants of God, Giovanni and
Francesco, by asking them one day to dine with
them : so these two soldiers of Jesus Christ accepted their charity, and took with them one of
their companions, Cecco, surnamed Il Boccia, who
sang many devout hymns, accompanying himself
on a viol; and after dinner, the ambassadors being
much edified by their conversation and manners,
they all went together to the Convent of Preaching
Friars at Camporeggi, and on their arrival the poor
ones of Jesus Christ sang hymns of praise, according
to their custom, and the twelve brothers gave them
welcome. And it pleased God that the Blessed

Giovanni and his companions should begin so to speak of that holy truth which gladdens every heart which thinks and speaks of it, that great desire thereto was kindled in the hearts of the Friars, and some wept, and others sighed.   Presently, Brother Cristofano Biagi, a man of learning and of good report, took the Blessed Giovanni into his cell, and at once gave him everything in it, his books, and all his wearing apparel, except what he had on him.   He emptied the room, till nothing was left but the mattress, and said Giovanni might give the things to whom he pleased.   These words were not spoken to deaf ears, for Giovanni and some of the others carried off all the things, and gave them away for the love of God.   After this, Friar Cristofano, accompanied by a lay brother, went about the city for two days, begging bread; and then, as if courting shame and reproach, he went to the new Abbey, to a certain brother Pietro, driving an ass before him with a load of dung, and having a basket full of dung hung round his neck, and so he went about the streets and squares, mortifying himself for the love of God. Furthermore, it pleased God that the charitable Giovanni and one of his companions, called Ambrogio, should go and stay with the above-named

8 *

Friars, and they discoursed so forcibly and eloquently on holy poverty, that by the mercy of Jesus Christ they were moved to such contrition, that most of them emptied their cells and gave away all their goods; some changed their dress for what was coarser and thicker; others preached Christ with marvellous fervour and godly wisdom; and there were some amongst them who received such enlightenment, that their own learning seemed to them as nothing in comparison with the spiritual light and truth that burst upon their minds; others wore very rough hair shirts. Any one who witnessed the operation of God in that convent would have been struck with astonishment, and a certain brother, who went there to mock at them, was smitten by Christ before he departed. Thus did a desire after holiness increase in this convent, of which many signs were observed by people living in the neighbourhood.

CHAPTER XXXIV.

An Exhortation to Conversion by the Blessed Giovanni.

HEREUPON the man of God Giovanni said that the grace of the Lord had come very near to man, and that Jesus Christ was showering on the world immeasurable gifts and blessings, especially in the revival and increase of religious orders and confraternities, so that in fervour of spirit he added: "Do not, my beloved ones, be careless or slothful, but hasten to meet this great gift of God with boundless charity,* excessive love, desire after holy poverty, and charity amongst yourselves; with joy, gladness and singing, and hearts emptied of all carnal and worldly affections. Christ never enters the soul that is occupied with other love than His; therefore spoil and empty your hearts, and clothe and fill yourselves with the dear and blessed Lord Jesus Christ, who, in giving Himself to you, will impart such delight to your souls that

* Che senta del pazzo.

they will be warmed and filled with joy unspeakable. Oh, blessing unperceived, lost and ignored by the miserable world! O ye blind and most foolish souls, who will not set yourselves to receive and taste the sweet and blessed Christ! Awake, you that sleep! rise up you that are like the dead! Christ will awake all people, inflame the coldest heart, and rekindle the dying embers. Go forth, then, bravely to the Blessed Christ, who is hastening to visit you."

CHAPTER XXXV.

How the Blessed Giovanni and his Brothers went to Pisa, Lucca, Pistoja, and Florence.

THE loving Giovanni was so zealous for God's honour, that when he was preaching the Divine Word, he feared neither cold, nor heat, nor storm; and once, in the middle of the winter, when snow was on the ground, he, not heeding the chilblains on his feet, went to Pisa with his devoted little company; and God worked a special miracle on their behalf, for as soon as their feet touched the snow, he and some of the others, who also had bad feet, were perfectly healed. As they went along they exhorted sinners to repent, and sang devout hymns. They took the road which went by the village of Cigoli, and here with great devotion was exposed a beautiful picture of our Lady, to whose protection they all lovingly recommended the venerable sisters of the before-mentioned Convent of Santa Bonda.

Another favour which God granted them was this : it took them nine days to reach Pisa, and though it very often rained during that time, their cloaks never got wet, nor did they take cold, or suffer the least inconvenience throughout the journey; except that the charitable Giovanni having, more for his brothers' sake than his own, taken some pitch with him, in case of insect bites, he was himself stung. So he said this had happened to him because he had not trusted in God, and that in future they would carry nothing whatever with them but the love of God deep down in their hearts.

In Pisa God so ordered it that they were turned away from the hospices, in order that the rich and good men of the place might give them welcome. And so it happened, for a noble and excellent citizen, who had four sons, distinguished merchants, showed much kindness to these poor men, keeping them all the time in his own house; and the alms given them were much more than they wished to receive, so they refused many offerings of money and clothing. They found there many virtuous people, both secular and religious, full of great and holy desires; and they saw, as people worthy of belief had already told them, that there were two hundred ladies in the city

who wore very rough hair garments, also many
gentlemen who used much self-mortification. According to their custom, they went about the city,
publicly preaching the salvation of souls, exhorting
persons in general and in particular to practise holiness and forsake sin; in this way giving much honour
and glory to Jesus Christ, and doing much good to
men. At last they, with their hosts, visited the Convent of Preaching Friars, and were much exhorted
and encouraged by their venerable and holy Prior to
continue their present way of life. He told them that
no one, be he man or woman, should, either from
error of judgment or false pride, desist from the
practice of holiness, or from speaking about God in
every place, adding : " Those who, in any place, refuse God when He wills their good, or for fear of
man turn from their true comfort, are fools; for
such people seem to think they know better than
God, which is the greatest folly. God Himself knows
best when to visit His spouse the soul, and he who
refuses Him then will not have Him when he seeks
Him." The poor ones of Jesus Christ were much
rejoiced at these words, and praising God and returning thanks to the brothers, they departed. Then they
took leave of their benefactors, and departing from

Pisa, they went, moved by the same charity, to the city of Lucca. Here also, as usual, they preached the Word of God, and went about the place praising the Name of Jesus Christ; and by the help of Divine grace they gathered there not a little fruit. Afterwards they came to Pistoja, doing and saying there what they thought would conduce to the honour of God and the salvation of men. Amongst those in that place, who, by the grace of God and their holy words, gave themselves wholly to Jesus Christ, were two who joined the company of poor ones, and became very zealous in God's service. One was called Pietro, and the other Paulino. And so, continuing their way, they passed through the magnificent city of Florence, singing and preaching Jesus Christ as they went along.

Throughout this journey Jesus Christ was so much honoured, and these poor brothers received such spiritual consolation, that the Blessed Giovanni said afterwards it was the happiest one he had taken for a long time.

CHAPTER XXXVI

*An Exhortation to Humility of Spirit by the Blessed
Giovanni.*

THE loving Giovanni said to his dear brothers:
"Let all worldly and anxious thoughts for
your kindred, or other vain things, give place to the
love of Christ, and let all your thoughts and words be
good and holy : in your conversation with each other
be careful to say nothing that could cause offence ;
take kindly and calmly what is said or done to you ;
let each of you seek to be the least, and consider
himself the worst ; think how much time you have
lost, and begin now to do well. Let us esteem others
better than ourselves, not murmuring, or finding
fault with others, for any cause. Let us grieve for
the sins we have committed against God, let us sym-
pathize with those who are afflicted, and weep with
those who weep ; let us mourn over a world which is
so ignorant of its true happiness that it refuses the

greatest good, and chooses the worst evil. Let us
help our neighbours, and constantly pray for them :
let us despise earthly things, and leaving them to the
world and its followers, let us set our hearts on the
high and great things of heaven and holiness. Finally,
let us strive to be Christ's disciples, and show that
we are such, by keeping the holy commandment He
left us, to love each other without measure. Let us
never be wanting in love—love as tender as that of
a son to his father, with the addition of unfeigned
humility. And last of all, when, by God's grace,
we have been enabled to do these things, we must
say, as our Blessed Lord commanded, 'We are useless and unprofitable servants;' for we have no
merit of our own, but God of His goodness allows
us to serve Him, that He might make us at length
His sons, and partakers of the joys of eternal life."

CHAPTER XXXVII.

How the Blessed Giovanni, with his Company, went to meet Pope Urban, at Viterbo.

N the return of the poor followers of Jesus Christ to Siena, they heard that the Holy Father, Pope Urban V., had arrived at Viterbo, from Avignon, with his court; and so the loyal-hearted Giovanni, and about seventy poor brothers whom he had gathered round him in less than two years, set out thither, to introduce themselves to the Holy Father, and to put themselves entirely under his direction, so that, by making the bishops of the Holy Church acquainted with their rule of life, all doubt about the lawfulness of the order might be removed.

At that time there dwelt in Siena a young man called Bianco di Santi : he belonged to Anciolina di Val d'Arno di Sopra, in the Duchy of Florence, but having from his childhood upwards been employed at Siena in the manufacture of wool, he was always called Bianco di Siena. He had often asked the Blessed Giovanni to receive him into his fraternity, but Giovanni seeing that he was a very beautiful and delicate-looking youth, and fearing that he would be unable to bear the severity of their rule, did not like to admit him. Now, when Bianco heard that the fervent Giovanni and most of his company were going to Viterbo, he left Siena immediately, and on reaching an inn, about three miles from the city, he waited for them there, ordering a plentiful repast to be prepared at his own expense. When Giovanni and his poor brothers came up to the place, Bianco went out to meet them, and affectionately and humbly prayed them to yield to his loving desire that they should rest there and dine, which they did; and when they had been somewhat refreshed by the good meal provided for them, Bianco fell on his knees, and with great vehemence implored the Blessed Giovanni and the others to receive him into their society. On which the beloved Giovanni, considering how his heart was set upon it, and how kindly he had treated them, consented to do so. Then they left that place, and continued their journey together.

CHAPTER XXXVIII

How they Arrived at Viterbo.

THROUGHOUT this journey, these poor followers of Jesus Christ had much honour and kindness shown them, especially in the States of Holy Church, and more alms were offered to them than they needed. It was esteemed a privilege to be able to offer them any hospitality, every one was anxious that they should eat or lodge at his own house, and they were looked upon as saints. At length they arrived at Viterbo, singing praises with great gladness.

First of all, they went to the principal church; then they sat down to eat in the market-place, and here they were surrounded by a great multitude, bringing them a wonderful supply of provisions. Both town and country people flocked eagerly to see them, and many were moved to tears by their devotion. While waiting here the arrival of the Holy

Father, they visited a nephew of Pope Urban, who
was then Abbot of Marseilles. He was very glad to
see them, and exhorted them to persevere in the service of God; and after they had taken their leave,
the Abbot sent them some money, which they refused,
however, at the same time thanking the donor.

Afterwards they visited the Count di Nola, who
was at that time governor of the patrimony: he
also was much pleased to see them, and offered them
large gifts.   One evening he invited the Blessed
Giovanni and some of his companions to sup with
him, and it being summer time, some lettuces were
laid on the table. But Giovanni, the man of God,
observed that the Count did not take any, and said,
"Do you not eat lettuces, Count?" to which the
Count replied, "I have not eaten any for fourteen
years, for I have a weak stomach, and lettuce dis-
agrees with me." Then, said the loving Giovanni,
"Take a little with us for friendship's sake;" and
the Count replied, "I would willingly do so, to please
this company, but it would make me ill." Again
Giovanni implored him to take some, for the love of
Christ and for their satisfaction. Then the Count,
seeing the anxiety of the Blessed Giovanni, took one
leaf, saying, as he did so, "Thou wilt make me have

a bad night." But no sooner had he eaten it, than his stomach was so strengthened, that he never felt any more pain, and from that time he was able to eat salad, or anything else, however cold or hard it might be.

CHAPTER XXXIX.

How they went to meet the Pope at Corneto.

WHEN the time drew near for the arrival of the Holy Father at Viterbo, Giovanni and his companions went to visit the cardinal legate of the church in that place, having been prevented from doing so before by his illness; after which Giovanni, Francesco Vincenti, and many of the poor brothers accompanied him to the Port of Corneto, where Pope Urban was to land, and there they were received with great honour. While they were there, they made themselves very useful in preparing for the worthy reception of the Holy Father, helping to make ready his bedchamber, and that of the cardinals. Then they went to the harbour, where a great wooden bridge, with triumphal decorations, was being built on the shore for the Sovereign Pontiff and his cardinals; and in this work they also helped as much as they could. Upon the approach of the Holy Father, almost every one was sent off the bridge except these poor brothers, all of whom, with olive branches in their hands and garlands of olive on their heads, stood waiting for him, some on the bridge, and some at its foot. As the Blessed Pope Urban and seven cardinals stepped on the bridge, the poor brothers raised shouts of joy, and cried out, "Blessed be Christ, and long live the Holy Father!" Giovanni, Francesco Vincenti, and some of their companions, humbly kissed his feet. These men were treated with the most wonderful respect and devotion, for though there were a great many prelates assembled, and not a few temporal lords, and notwithstanding the great crowd of people, room was always made for them: they walked close to the Holy Father, and two of them carried the banner under which he rode. On reaching Corneto, he dismounted at the Convent of the Friars Minor, amidst shoutings and rejoicings; but the greatest and most wonderful novelty of that day was the presence of those fervent and lowly men, and many letters were written about this new and holy society, and sent to different parts of Christendom. When the Holy Father heard of them, he said he should like to talk with them, and encourage them in their holy life; but the foreign

9 *

bishops and ambassadors were so angry at this, that he was not able to do so. However, the poor brothers visited the Cardinal of Avignon, who was the Pope's brother. He showed them great kindness, giving them comfort and counsel, and offering to be their protector and father, which made the Blessed Giovanni say that he was like a lamb for his meekness and gentleness. Francesco Bruni, of Florence, secretary to the Holy Father, also treated them very kindly.

CHAPTER XL

*How they accompanied the Pope from Corneto to Vi-
terbo, and how the religious Habit was promised to
them.*

THE entry into Corneto of the Holy Father,
Pope Urban, took place on Friday, the 4th
of June, A.D. 1567. The Monday following he rode
towards Viterbo, accompanied by the poor brothers,
who almost ran by his side, for he rode fast. The
Holy Father considerately sent word to them to come
on at their ease, on which the ardent Francesco,
wishing to be obedient, said, "I am at my ease if I
can come close to him, hear him, and touch him."
Then he ran on in front, so that he might kiss his
feet when he passed. And such was the kindness
of the Sovereign Pontiff, that when he saw him
kneeling on the ground, he stopped his horse, and
allowed Francesco to kiss and touch him, and twice
on crossing over water, the devoted Francesco held

up his robes. On reaching Toscanella, the Holy Father dismounted, and on Tuesday evening he sent one of his courtiers to fetch the poor brothers, who said to them, " I bring you good news: come to the Pope." They joyfully obeyed, and going to the monastery of the Friars Minor, they awaited him there. Presently there appeared a venerable man, who said to Francesco Vincenti, "Come to the Holy Father," and led him into his presence. On entering the room, Francesco laid his old cloak on the ground and knelt down ; and when the Blessed Pope Urban told him to come close to him, Francesco humbly knelt at his feet, while the Holy Father, full of wonder and admiration, questioned him on their rule of life, and the motives which led them to it; adding, that he did not like their having such variety of dress amongst them, but he would give them a habit: they might wear hoods, and he wished them to continue to go barefoot. In reply to this Francesco began by saying what a happiness he felt it to be in the presence of the Holy Father, and then briefly told him what were the motives which induced them to undertake their present life. This interview lasted some time, and before it ended the Blessed Pope Urban gave orders to one of his servants that all the poor brothers who were on the shore when he landed should be clothed in white. In conclusion, the fervent Francesco said that they put themselves under the authority of the Pope, and were anxious to devote their lives to the Holy Church and to his service : they would be content to wear long robes or hoods, or anything he pleased. He also begged that his Holiness would quite understand that they fully intended to serve him lovingly and faithfully. These words pleased the Holy Father not a little, and the devoted Francesco, having received his blessing, took his leave, and joyfully related everything to Giovanni and his companions. On Wednesday morning, the 9th of June, the Blessed Pope Urban made his pontifical entry into Viterbo with great pomp and magnificence, attended by eight cardinals, a number of bishops and other dignitaries, and many nobles and ambassadors, while praises and shouts of joy resounded on all sides, so that it seemed as if the very stones cried out, "Benedictus qui venit in Nomine Domini."

CHAPTER XLI.

How they were Accused of Heresy in Viterbo.

AFTER these poor brothers had followed the Holy Father to Viterbo with great devotion and reverence, God permitted their faith to be tried, in order that the purity and holiness of their lives might shine forth more clearly; and He allowed the devil to tempt many prelates and other religious with his malicious suggestions, putting it into their heads that these poor men held the pernicious and heretical opinions of the Fraticelli. For this reason some of the cardinals and bishops, and certain Mendicant Friars who did not really know the poor brothers, suspected them of heresy, and spoke against them to the Holy Father, defaming and slandering them. Many of the courtiers also hated them, and spoke evil of them, but by the Blessed Pope Urban, and his brother the Cardinal of Avignon, and all who knew them well, they were not only loved and honoured, but also openly commended and protected. This persecution obliged them to exercise much patience, humility, and many other virtues, and they had so much to endure, that some of them would not bear it, left the congregation, and returned to the miserable world. The loving Giovanni and the other brave soldiers of Christ were very much grieved at this departure, for they feared for the salvation of those who left them; but their own injuries gave them no uneasiness, for they trusted in God for help, and in the testimony of their pure consciences, knowing too that "it is through much tribulation we must enter into the kingdom of God;" and that "God is faithful, Who will not suffer us to be tempted above that we are able." They were not surprised at their persecution, when they learnt what they were ignorant of at the time they determined to wait on the Pope; viz., the heresies which had crept in upon the state of holy poverty, and were still arising. Then was fulfilled that which a holy man called Il Nero, of the city of Castello, had prophesied about them,—that they would have to cross a great river, and that this would show which of them were of God, for many of them would obediently cross it, and some would refuse to do so : and so it happened. But the just God very soon manifested His displeasure against those who had left the congregation of poor ones, for on returning to the world, they were detested by almost everybody : and during the persecution God worked a singular miracle, in the case of two Aretini (men of Arezzo), who had previously given up their possessions, and together joined the congregation. One of them, called Se Biliotto, was the first to leave, and he was hung at Arezzo, in company with fourteen others; and on the same day, in Viterbo, the other one, who was called Pietrino, and had remained in the brotherhood, rendered up his spirit to God in great fervour and devotion.

CHAPTER XLII

An Exhortation to Perseverance by the Blessed Giovanni.

OR this cause, Giovanni, being full of faith, said to his patient companions: "Behold the working of Divine Justice, how fearful it is; see how God wills that the flour should be discerned from the bran. Yet this need not dishearten us, because even some of the angels fell from heaven, and those who remained were perfected; and in all holy congregations there have been some who wanted perseverance. And so I believe it will be with us; but woe to him who goes out from us! God wishes to prove who are serving Him faithfully, and who are not, so that no one may deceitfully shelter himself under His cloak. Therefore rejoice, and take comfort in this, that you have remained on His side, and have not joined those who, being deprived of the grace of our Lord, have returned to the miserable world, to the abominations of a sinful life, accompanied by such disgrace and shame, that few will have anything to do with them. Let us therefore learn wisdom at their expense, and at the same time have compassion on them, and pray for them, and be watchful over ourselves. Let us, my beloved brethren, persevere bravely if we would not be discomfited and confounded; for he who runs away, instead of fighting bravely, can have no right to the crown of victory; and in this battle none are defeated against their will, for our enemy is no stronger than we are. Be humble, then, and patient, so that all may know you to be disciples and servants of Jesus Christ."

CHAPTER XLIII.

*How they were Examined by the Inquisitor on their
Heretical Depravity, and being found Pious and
Religious, the Pope gave them the Habit.*

AS the ill-treatment of the poor brothers continued, and so many complaints of them were made to the Blessed Urban, he ordered the Cardinal of Marseilles, who was one of the Preaching Friars, and learned in theology, to examine them strictly, although his brother the Cardinal of Avignon advised him to the contrary, as they were simple and unlearned men; and he feared lest, out of very ignorance, they might say something which would be considered heretical. However, the men themselves were very eager to be examined, and so one morning the Cardinal of Marseilles sent for them; and in the presence of a notary, who had prepared a blank sheet of paper, he and the Inquisitor began to examine them very carefully, asking them a great many questions; but the Blessed Jesus Christ, Who is infinite truth and wisdom, so enlightened their minds, that they were enabled to give a right answer to everything, according to the Catholic Faith and the decrees of the Holy Roman Church; such being their intention.   And they spoke so eloquently of their poverty and holy purpose, that the cardinal was full of admiration; and so there seemed nothing to write against them.   The cardinal invited them to his table that morning and the following, when he treated them as his own sons, waiting on them himself.   He gave such a good report of them to the Blessed Pope Urban, that whereas he had at first procured enough white cloth for twenty-five of their number, he now wished to clothe them all, and ordered sixty robes, and as many hoods of the same colour, to be made for them; and besides that, he gave them money out of his treasury for their support, all which they respectfully received.   All the brothers who were at the Papal Court were then clothed in white, and the Holy Father ordered robes to be sent to those who were absent, which was done by the Blessed Giovanni, who also wrote thus: "Let those who have courage to persevere to the end, accept this habit, and with God's blessing devoutly put it on; but let not him accept it who is irresolute and fearful, for woe to him who wears it under false pretences; woe to him!"

The Cardinal of Marseilles, who had at first looked suspiciously on them, being doubtful as to their opinions, afterwards became their benefactor and protector, and he took them to hear Mass in the Pope's Chapel, on S. John Baptist's day, and on the day of the blessed Apostles S. Peter and S. Paul. He also commanded them to attend the solemn Mass of the Blessed Pope Urban in the same chapel, which they did; and to these poor men it appeared almost heavenly. The cardinal likewise cleverly and effectually silenced certain masters in theology and Mendicant Friars, who disapproved of the poverty of these men; and he told a chaplain and secretary of the Cardinal of Avignon, who was also friendly to them, that if necessary he would die in their defence; and wherever he went, he praised them and took their part. But many who spoke against them, when they understood their pure and holy intention, held them in devotion and respect, and so their character was continually being cleared. Almost every one rejoiced when the Blessed Pope Urban had invested them with cassocks and hoods, and they magnified the Name of Jesus Christ, and blessed the Holy Father for his gift, and the men were called throughout the province "the Pope's poor." Other cardinals and lords also welcomed them to their houses, and showed them much honour, so that, as they said afterwards, it seemed sometimes as if they themselves were cardinals. Monsignor of Marseilles was their chief friend, and he invited them to his table so often, that another cardinal used to call them the esquires of the Cardinal of Marseilles.

CHAPTER XLIV

Of the reasons which induced them to remain awhile in Viterbo, and how, when they left that place, they went to the Lake of Bolsena.

HE poor brothers remained in Viterbo for some days after the Habit had been given them, for three special reasons. First, that they might be fully informed of the will of the Holy Father concerning their manner of life, so as to advance still further in God's service, by conforming themselves always to the decrees and constitutions of the Holy Church, and they learnt much on this point from the prelates of the court—especially the Cardinal of Avignon—who gave them full information on every matter connected with their life. And on the part of the Holy Father, he told them not to keep all together, for a multitude causes confusion and disorder, but to disperse themselves about in the cities or villages of their neighbourhood, as they thought best,

10

always with the consent of the bishops of those provinces: they were also cautioned against holding the opinions of the Fraticelli. These instructions were gratefully received by the poor brothers. Their second reason for remaining with the court was, that their pure and holy design might become better and more generally known ; and the third reason was that they might see their particular Father, Monsignor Buccio, Bishop of Castello, who had written to tell them that he was coming to court that day.

But when they heard that for some good reason he was unable to come, they paid a farewell visit to his Holiness, Pope Urban, who promised them every support and assistance, and with loving words exhorted them to persevere in their holy life : and after receiving his blessing they took leave of him. He also gave them enough money to buy six ells of cloth, which would be sufficient to make five Habits. They also paid farewell visits to the cardinals and other prelates, and the Cardinals of Avignon and Marseilles gave them much additional comfort and encouragement, by tendering them all the help in their power. Yet notwithstanding all these offers of help from the Holy Father, and cardinals, and their other friends, they would not ask for a Papal Bull, or any exemption whatever, for they wished in everything to keep the commandments and counsels of the Holy Gospel, and humbly to obey the pastors of the Holy Church. Besides which, the Bishop of Castello, in two later letters, had advised them to this effect: "Trust to virtue for your defence, and not to Papal Bulls." Other bishops who loved them, also, counselled them not to ask for any privilege whatever. And so these poor humble-minded men, clothed in white, took their departure from Viterbo, and with loud voices, praising Jesus Christ, they went on their way till they came to the Lake of Bolsena, where there is a convent for women, called the Convent of S. Mary Magdalen; and Giovanni being very much devoted to that saint, and it being the day of her Feast, he and his devout company went to that Church to hear the Divine Office, and were gladly and lovingly welcomed there.

CHAPTER XLV.

How Giovanni, being seized with Fever at the Lake of
Bolsena, was carried to Acquapendente.

OW it came to pass that the merciful God,
seeing how nobly His brave soldier Giovanni
had borne the fight, and how many pains of mind
and body he had endured for' His sake, and seeing
too that the poor brothers had received the Habit from
the Pope, and were fully instructed in all things necessary for their welfare, He resolved to give Giovanni
the crown of victory, and transplant him to eternal
rest.   So the same day Giovanni was seized with a
burning fever, at which this patient man was greatly
rejoiced, perceiving that it was God's visitation.   His
brothers and sons in Christ were full of sorrow, however, and fearing that his sickness might increase in
that place, they bore him to Acquapendente, and
there used every possible means to cure him.   But as
his sickness increased, the most faithful Giovanni was

anxious to make his confession once more, and to receive the Viaticum of the Body of Christ. On the arrival of the priest with the Blessed Sacrament, Giovanni humbly prayed Benedetto di Pace, of the city of Castello, one of his most zealous companions, to write down the words he spoke, a copy of which is contained in the following chapter.

CHAPTER XLVI.

The last Will and Testament of the Blessed Giovanni.

IN THE NAME OF OUR LORD JESUS CHRIST CRUCIFIED. AMEN.

IN the year of our Lord 1357, in the 5th Indiction, on the 26th day of July, Urban the Fifth being the reigning Pope. Be it known to all who shall behold this writing, that the good and venerable Giovanni di Pietro Colombini of Siena, being very infirm in body, but in full possession of his senses, humbly kneeling before the most Holy Body of Christ, Which was held in the hands of the priest Giovanni di Schiavo, rector of the Church of S. Angiolo at Acquapendente, in the presence of witnesses, and of me, the undersigned notary, dictated these words :—

I, Giovanni, in the presence of my Lord Jesus Christ, confess that I have been ungrateful to God for the blessings He has conferred upon me; that I am the greatest sinner in the world, and for my evil deeds am deserving of hell-fire : nevertheless, trust-

ing in God's mercy, I hope that He will be gracious
to me, and grant me eternal life.

I do in very deed and truth confess and believe
in God the Father, the Son, and Holy Ghost, and
in all that the Holy Mother Church of Rome, and
her pastors, Pope Urban, the cardinals his brothers,
and the other bishops of the Church believe. And
I declare that the life I have led since I embraced
poverty, to the present time, has been and is for the
glory of my Lord Jesus Christ, and the honour and
advancement of the Holy Church of God, and her
most holy and blessed Father and Ruler, Pope Urban
the Fifth, the cardinals his brothers, and the other
bishops and governors, to whom, being Christ's
vicars upon earth, I have always, and will be obedient until death. I affirm that this is the way of
salvation, and that whoever wanders therefrom, and
does not fully believe what is ordered and determined by the aforesaid Pastors to be the work of
God by the inspiration of the Holy Ghost, and is not
obedient, is not a true Catholic Christian : and I believe and am sure that whoever errs in this respect
is separated from Christ. But if I have in ignorance
said or done anything which is contrary to the will of
the said holy Pastors, I repent of it, and confess my

fault, and demand of you, Giovanni the priest, the sacrament of penance; although I do not know that I have ever failed on these points. I place myself entirely, both body and soul, in the bosom of the Holy Church and her Pastors, and so I hope for eternal life. And I exhort my companions, absent as well as present, who have hitherto been faithful to Holy Mother Church, and to her Pastors, never to separate from her, for in doing so they would be departing from the Blessed Christ. Furthermore, as goodness is very often envied, and persecuted, and my conscience urges me to vindicate the truth, I affirm, respecting the convent of SS. Abbundio and Abbundanzio, near Siena, where I have placed my daughter and other relations of mine, and where I and my companions have often lodged, for the sake of the good and holy instructions we have received from the sisters dwelling there, that these sisters are the holiest, the most pure, the most devoted to Holy Mother Church, and the most upright in the whole world; full of penance, charity, and almsgiving; very poor in spirit, possessing no private wealth, though they are rich in common. I consider them all to be saints.

Executed at Acquapendente, in the patrimony, in the house of Ambrogio di Gianni of that place, in the presence of the undersigned Ambrogio, Benedetto di Conte, Simone d'Agnoluccio of Perugia, Bartoluccio di Santi of the city of Castello, Seculars ; Francesco di Mino Vincenti, Giovanni di Geri, Bianco di Santi of Siena, and Simon di Muccio of Monterelli, all cited to be witnesses: the aforesaid Giovanni praying me, the undersigned notary, to make a public writing of the same ; and I, Benedetto di Pace, of the city of Castello, by imperial authority judge in ordinary and notary public, being present, have attested and written down these words, publishing them, and setting my seal and name thereto.

CHAPTER XLVII.

How he was borne in his sickness to the Abbey of S. Salvatore.

HEN the faithful Giovanni had concluded these sayings, he received the Most Holy Body of Christ with such devotion, that all who were present shed tears at the sight. Afterwards, his loving companions being anxious to take him, while yet alive, to his beloved convent of Santa Bonda, carried him as far as the village where was the Abbey of S. Salvatore; and many people followed them all along the road, for they were very desirous to see this servant of God, and to help him, if possible. On reaching the village, he was taken to the house of a good man, called Naddo di Vanni, who had always hospitably received these poor men whenever they came to the place, and here Giovanni grew so much worse that he could not be moved again. Perceiving that his death was drawing near, he gave directions for his burial, and declared his last wishes, praying the before-named Benedetto to write this down also, a copy of which is contained in the following chapter.

CHAPTER XLVIII.

The Blessed Giovanni's Directions concerning his Burial.

IN THE NAME OF OUR CRUCIFIED LORD JESUS CHRIST. AMEN.
IN THE YEAR OF OUR LORD 1367, THE 29TH DAY OF JULY, IN THE 5TH
INDICTION, IN THE TIME OF POPE URBAN V.

BE it known to all who shall behold this writing, that the good and venerable Giovanni di Pietro Colombini, a citizen of Siena, being weak in body but sound in mind, I, the undersigned notary, in the presence of witnesses, asked him where he would like to be buried, if it should please God to take his life; and he replied that, if he should die (and he told me and the witnesses to bear this in mind), he wished to be buried near the boundary wall of the Convent and Cloister of SS. Abbundio and Abbundanzio at Siena, by the door of the kitchen garden belonging to the convent: that his dead body was to be wrapped up in canvas, the hands tied behind, and he was to be taken thither on the back of an ass. These he said were his last wishes, and he told me, the notary, to record them in writing.

Executed in the village adjoining the Abbey of S. Salvatore, in the province of Siena, in the house of Naddo di Vanni; in the presence of Naddo di Guglielmo, of the aforesaid place, and of Fazio di Betto of Montalcino, Gualtieri di Pietro of Siena, Donato di Giovanni e Santori, surnamed Romeo, of the city of Puligniano, in the kingdom of Apulia, cited as witnesses; and I, Benedetto di Pace, of the city of Castello, being requested to do so, recorded the above, and set my seal and name thereto.

CHAPTER XLIX.

A very Holy and Edifying Exhortation delivered by the Blessed Giovanni in his last Sickness.

GIOVANNI, the man of God, having declared his last wishes, began most affectionately to exhort his beloved companions, and he said to them : "Oh, dearest fathers and brothers in Jesus Christ, you see that God wishes to take me to Himself, and it is our duty cheerfully to submit to His Will, for He is the Giver of life and death, and what He lays upon us is for our good, and the salvation of our souls. You need not be afraid of that happening which is spoken of in Holy Scripture, 'I will strike the shepherd, and the sheep shall be dispersed,' for I am not a good shepherd, on account of my ignorance. I know not even how to govern myself, much less others; and I deserve to be punished, but in the kindness of your hearts you have borne with me. Besides, there are many amongst you who are capable of governing, and I especially recommend Francesco.Vincenti to you for that office: he is more worthy of it than I am, and will be your father and ruler. Follow and obey him, and ·do not forsake his guidance, for he will lead you in the right way. And I earnestly beseech you all, absent as well as present, for the sake of the Blessed Jesus Christ, to pardon me if I have failed in my duty towards you, if I have foolishly corrected you too much or too little, or have given you any cause for offence ; and if so, I ask your forgiveness (I would do so on my knees if I could) for the sake of Christ crucified. And I implore you to love each other, and always live peaceably together, no one wishing to be above his fellow, for he who will be greatest shall be the least, and he that humbles himself shall be exalted. Study as much as possible to follow the example of Jesus Christ and the holy apostles, and when your works are done after that pattern then you will be true Gesuati. Let your every thought, word, and deed, be for the honour and glory of Jesus Christ. Whatever you may be doing, let His holy Name be ever in your heart and mouth ; and I implore you to persevere unto the end, for he who only begins well will not be saved, but he who perseveres. Be brave soldiers of Jesus Christ, and by His help triumph over the world, the flesh, and the devil.

'God is faithful, who will not suffer you to be tempted above that which you are able.' The labour of the battle is of short duration, but the crown of victory is perpetual: you have only to bear this penance for a little while, for death comes quickly upon us all. Learn, dearly beloved, how to make the most of your time, that death may not find you unprepared. Again, I tell you that if you persevere in the way you have begun, you will increase in merit and in number, every one will love and respect you, and you will never want for any necessary thing. When your wants are supplied, give thanks to God, and pray for your benefactors; and when you are not so well off, have patience, and put your trust in Jesus Christ. He will speedily help you, for He never forsakes His faithful servants. In all your sorrows and adversities also have faith and hope in God. See how often the Divine Goodness has helped us, and particularly observe how this saying of the gospel has been anew fulfilled in us, 'When you shall be brought before councils, do not think beforehand what you have to say, for it shall be given you from above.' When the chief prelates of the court unjustly accused us to the Blessed Pope Urban, and he ordered us to be examined by men of great learning and authority, we foolish and unlearned men were enabled by God to answer so correctly, that instead of being shamefully condemned, as many thought we should be, we were honourably rewarded: men's hatred towards us was turned into love; those who sought to injure us were the cause of our being benefited; and his Holiness, being convinced of our innocence and purity, gave white Habits to all of us, not only those who were present, but the absent ones also. You are bound, therefore, to do your very utmost for the glory of God and Holy Church. Try to have your souls whiter than your Habits, by keeping your hearts pure, confessing frequently, and receiving the Most Holy Sacrament of the Body of Christ at Easter, and on other great feasts. Be joyful, and serve the Lord with gladness; love each other as brethren; and when any of your companions are sick, tend them as lovingly as possible, as you would Jesus Christ Himself, for He says in the Holy Gospel, 'What you do to one of the least of mine, you do it to me.' Spend your time usefully; take care that the enemy does not find you idle, but always occupied in some good work. In all your labours let some holy thought find a place in your heart; read, or listen to the reading of spiritual books; be constant in prayer by day and night; meditate on the justice and mercy of God, in order that you

11

may love and fear Him. Think over your sins with heartfelt sorrow, and accuse yourselves of them to God with simplicity, humbly asking for pardon : think how miserably prone we are to fall, and how good God is in raising us up again. Meditate often on the hour of death, the day of judgment, the punishment of the damned, and the glory of the blessed ; think of the general and special blessings you have received from God, and thank Him heartily for all; and above all keep in mind the holy life and Passion of Jesus Christ. This enlightens and fortifies the devout soul, and is the best medicine for all our spiritual infirmities. Contemplate also the lives and sufferings of the saints: this will help us to despise vicious practices, and all sensual and worldly pleasures, and kindle in our hearts a desire after holiness, and a willingness to suffer for Jesus Christ's sake, for ' through many tribulations we must enter into the kingdom of God.' Be sure, my beloved brethren, that you cannot enter heaven by any other way : therefore fight bravely, and as much as possible strive after God's glory and the salvation of your souls, so that, when this short life is over, the Blessed Christ may grant you eternal glory."

CHAPTER L.

HEN turning to Francesco Vincenti, he said to him in the tenderest accents : " Oh, my dear brother, thou knowest how long we have loved one another, not from any relationship between us, but solely in God. For the sake of Christ crucified, I commend to you our spiritual fathers and sons, whom God has committed to our charge. See how fully they have trusted us, believing us to be good servants of God. They give up their own will entirely, and obey us in all things ; they have forsaken their relations, friends, and everything they have in the world : therefore we are bound to take care of them, as if they were our own, for we shall have to give account of them to our just Judge. I entreat you to watch over them, be the good father and shepherd of their souls, their master and brother both in doc-

11 *

trine and example, so that by God's help, and thy love and care, they may attain a happy end."

Francesco, full of sorrow, answered him with sobs : "Thy loving words break my heart, not because I am unwilling to bear any fatigue, or do all in my power for the welfare of our poor companions, as I am in duty bound, but deprived of thy dear companionship, my life will henceforth be a continual death ; and, besides that, not being capable of governing them, they will derive very little benefit from my rule. For these reasons, therefore, I implore thee, as thou lovest me, to intercede for me with Jesus Christ, that He will soon remove me from this mortal life." He made this request so humbly, that the loving Giovanni promised to pray that God would grant him this desire.

Then the Blessed Giovanni requested all those present to withdraw, except the priest Giovanni di Schiavo ; and calling him to his side, he revealed to him in confidence many things which were going to happen, and asked him to make them known to Madonna Paola, the venerable Abbess of the Convent of Santa Bonda. After this the others returned, and assembled round his bed, and although the loving Giovanni was so exhausted that he could hardly speak, he forced himself to do so, out of the love he bore to his companions; and looking at Francesco Vincenti, he said to him: "Oh, my dear brother, I may no longer be with thee; again I recommend this our family to thy care, and although I believe that thou wilt not long survive me, I still entreat thee to watch over them."

Then turning to his other spiritual children, of whom about twenty were present, the rest having been sent, some to Siena, some to other places, he said: "Oh, my dear sons and brothers, I have not deserved to be the father of such a good family, but so it is. I have loved you much, and have indeed desired the salvation of your souls. I would willingly have died for you a hundred times a day, if such had been possible. Again I exhort you to continue in the way you have begun, and again I ask your forgiveness if I have given you any cause of offence. I bless you all, absent as well as present, also those who shall in future join our holy society, and persevere unto death." Then he made the sign of the cross over them, saying, "God the Father, Son, and Holy Ghost, bless you."

CHAPTER LI.

The Last Exhortation of the Blessed Giovanni.

ON hearing these loving words of their master and father, Francesco and the other poor ones were overcome with grief, and perceiving that death was drawing near, they began to weep; and although they restrained themselves as much as possible in his presence, for fear of distressing him, Giovanni saw their tears, and said: "Do not weep for me, dear brothers, for I trust that God will not leave me, nor I Him; not for my merits, but of His infinite mercy. So do not grieve at my departure, for I believe that I am going to a place where I shall help you in future better than I have in times past. You are not born of my confidence, but of God; hope then in Him, and put your trust in Him; and if you love me do not weep, but rather rejoice that I go to our Saviour Jesus, who of His mercy has given us His Name; therefore, whether we will or no, we are called

Gesuati. Besides, you know what Jesus said to His Father, 'I will, Father, that where I am, there shall my servant be;'" and so, if we serve Him faithfully, we shall all spend eternal life with Him, not in sadness and weeping, but in perpetual happiness and glory. One thing more I ask of you, and for love's sake I command you, and that is, that you should take the Convent and the sisters of Santa Bonda under your protection. You remember I have said in my will that I wish to be buried there, because I know their holy and praiseworthy life. I should have thought myself highly favoured if it had pleased God to allow me to die in that devout place, but because I am not worthy of it, or for some other reason, such has not been God's Will. Therefore, as far as in me lies, I commend this convent to your care. When you can do them any good, do so; and when you want anything of them, do not be afraid of asking it, for they are very charitable, as most of you already know. But do not be too familiar either with that or any other convent of women, and as a rule be reserved with all women, and be very prudent and discreet in your conversation with them, not because I mistrust either you or them, but to avoid any cause for scandal. As I said before, I believe all the sisters of Santa Bonda to be saints, and therefore, when you go there, ask them to pray for me. And I pray thee, Francesco, that as we have been of one mind ever since we resolved to embrace poverty for the sake of Jesus Christ, so we may still be so in our burial, and that thou wilt be buried in the same place with me;" and with many tears Francesco promised that it should be so. Then, once more gathering up his remaining strength, the loving-hearted Giovanni gave them all his blessing.

CHAPTER LII

*How the Blessed Giovanni received Extreme Unction
and the Recommendation of the Soul, and how he
Died.*

THEN after the manner of a faithful Christian
he demanded the Holy Sacrament of Extreme
Unction, which he received most devoutly, being then
perfectly conscious; and as his death drew near, his
brothers knelt around his bed, and heartily prayed
God to have mercy on his soul. The priest said the
Office for the Recommendation of the Soul, and some
other prayers, and lastly read to him the Passion of
Jesus Christ from the Holy Gospel; and when he
came to the words, *Pater, in manus tuas commendo
spiritum meum,* that blessed soul was released from
the body, and went, we fully believe, to the glory of
eternal life. This happened on Saturday, the last day
of July, in the year of our Lord 1367. And although
we ought not to mourn when holy men depart from

this mortal life to the immortal, yet as soon as the Blessed Giovanni was dead, there arose great lamentation amongst his sons, because their beloved father was lost to them in the flesh. Francesco Vincenti, especially, was overwhelmed with grief; he threw himself on Giovanni's neck, and kissing him all over, he cried out: "Oh, my Father Giovanni, why hast thou left me? Is this the companionship I hoped for from thee? To whom can I turn now for advice and support? From whom else shall I ever gain such comfort as I have from thee? Thou wast my good master and father, thou didst enlighten my mind, inflame my affections, and guide me always in the right way. Oh, dear Giovanni, I weep not for thee, but for myself; thou art gone to happiness, I am left behind to lament; I rejoice much in thy bliss, but grieve over my misery. Oh, most loving Giovanni, of thy charity, I earnestly implore thee to ask God soon to take me from this darkness, and let me join thee in perpetual light. When will the hour come that I shall find myself with thee?" Having said these and other words, the good Francesco embraced him again, and with many tears kissed his hands and face. All the other poor brothers also poured forth their lamentations, each one relating the great benefits and loving ministrations he had received from Giovanni; and this lasted for more than an hour. Afterwards, when their weeping was a little moderated, they saw that their Father Francesco was still so overcome with grief, that he could not restrain his tears; and they tried to persuade him to leave the Blessed Giovanni's body, but in vain. So they took him by force, and raised him upright on his feet, and then withdrew from him a little, for it seemed as if his heart would break with grief. Lastly, these poor brothers, with sighs and tears approaching in order the body of the Blessed Giovanni, kissed his hand, as if he had been a priest, with much reverence and devotion.

CHAPTER LIII.

How the Body of the Blessed Giovanni was borne to the Convent of Santa Bonda.

AFTER this, they questioned amongst themselves whether they were obliged to carry that holy body to the grave in the ignominious way he had desired in his will; and being distressed at the thought of such disrespect, they took counsel thereon with certain good men, who all agreed that they were not bound to treat his body with such contempt as he in his humility had ordained, but that they should bury him with all the honour which his holy life deserved : and this being settled, they decided on carrying him to the Convent of Santa Bonda, where he wished to be buried, and with many tears they removed him from the house where he had died. All the people of the country round, both men and women, came to see him, and to kiss his hand devoutly, as if he had been a priest; and the Abbot and community of S. Salvadore sent many wax candles. His body having been reverently put into a coffin, they devoutly carried him forth, being accompanied for some distance by almost the whole neighbourhood, many of whom followed him as far as the confines of the territory, and in all the places through which they passed people came out to see him; and in this way that holy body was borne with much reverence and devotion to the village of San Quirino, where they rested for a little while. At last they reached the before-named Convent of Santa Bonda, where the holy body was placed in the church, and exposed to view.

CHAPTER LIV.

How many holy Women wept over the Body of the Blessed Giovanni in the Convent of Santa Bonda.

WHEN Madonna Paola and Sister Bartolommea and the other devout nuns saw that the Blessed Giovanni, whose life they had earnestly hoped for, was dead, they burst into tears, and bitterly lamented being deprived of the spiritual consolation of their venerable father. Each one spoke of his holy words and works, and chiefly of the great love which for the glory of God and their own salvation he had shown towards them; and in the midst of their weeping they never ceased talking of the great benefits they had received from him. Then the brothers sent word to all their companions who were within reach, so they came immediately, and when they saw the venerable body of their beloved father, they mourned as the others had done. When the news reached Siena, almost the whole city wept, and not only the Blessed Giovanni's relations and friends, but nearly every one went to see him.

Madonna Biagia, the holy wife of the Blessed Giovanni, came to the convent, full of sorrow, with many of her relations and friends, and when she saw the holy body of her dearly-loved Giovanni, she threw herself upon him, and weeping bitterly, said, in piteous tones: " Oh, most chaste and holy face, which for the sake of Christ I have refrained from kissing for twelve years ! Oh, holy eyes, how many tears you have shed for Christ crucified ! Oh, sweet mouth, which preached so fervently for God's glory and the salvation of souls, and so tenderly comforted those in sorrow, comfort me, who am afflicted beyond all other Siennese women. I do not mourn *thy* death, but *mine*, being deprived of thee, my life. Thou art living in the glory of the heavenly country, but I am dead in the misery of this wretched world. I deserve more pity than all other afflicted widows, for I am deprived of the best and holiest husband in all Siena." Then devoutly kissing his hands, she said: "Oh, blessed hands, what large alms you have given to the poor ! what menial offices have been done by you! what loving letters you have written! and all out of love to your Creator !" Likewise, kissing his feet, she said, in broken accents: "Oh, feet, so delicate formerly, when covered, that even the seams of your stockings hurt you, yet afterwards, when you went barefoot for the sake of Christ, you cared not for wounds from stones, or thorns, or for bitter cold;" and then earnestly gazing on him, she said, with sobs and tears, "Oh, most tender, weak, and delicate body, which was enabled by Divine strength gladly to endure what was impossible for human strength. Oh, Colombini, pure and chaste, filled with the fire of the Holy Ghost, now is the favour granted thee which thou hast longed for so many years, to die in preaching the Name of Christ." And turning to Caterina di Colombini, she said: "Oh, dearest sister, who with thy tongue didst pierce the heart of our lord and father, Giovanni, saying to him, when he left Siena, 'May the Lord protect thee,' He has cared for him so much that He allowed him by excessive suffering, both of body and mind, to die for Him."

Caterina and his other relations and friends also mourned for him, and one of them, Alissa de Bandinelli, when she saw the precious body of the Blessed Giovanni, said, with tears: "Now is that light extinguished from our view, which I saw when thou prayedst so fervently in thy chamber. Who will now

help me in the work of my salvation ? How affectionately, dearest father, didst thou exhort me to live
to God's glory ! How earnestly didst thou write to me
that I should love Jesus Christ more than my sons,
saying that my children could not admit me to eternal
life ! I entreat thee, for Jesus Christ's sake, Whom
thou lovedst so much, to intercede with Him for
myself and my sons." Thus did all his relations
and friends mourn and weep over his body, remembering how beneficial had been his life and teaching,
and every one devoutly kissed his hand.

CHAPTER LV.

Of the Burial of the Blessed Giovanni.

B Y the time that their weeping was somewhat abated, all was ready for the funeral, and the priests, both secular and religious, a great number of whom were present, began devoutly to chant the Divine Office, and reverently performed all the ceremonies, as if the Blessed Giovanni had been a priest. Then his companions, about forty of whom were there, being all clothed in the Habit given by the Holy Father, took the coffin containing that holy body, which looked more as if it was asleep than dead, and with sighs and tears laid it in the grave they had prepared in the church near the entrance to the cloister; and after covering it with many flowers and sweet-smelling herbs, they replaced the earth and the pavement. This was on Monday, the third of August, A.D. 1367. This being done, the holy wife of the Blessed Giovanni talked for a while with the sisters, commending to them, with many tears, the soul of her beloved Giovanni, and entreating them to pray for him, although she believed that he had entered into life eternal. To Madonna Paola she said: "For the sake of the devoted love you in this convent show to my husband's memory, you need not be afraid to ask anything of me, for I will gladly do for you all that is in my power." The venerable Abbess could hardly speak for her tears, but she answered: "We rejoice greatly that you should commend the soul of the Blessed Giovanni to our prayers, although it is needless, for it is far dearer to us than our own souls. Oh, that we might be where he is! We thank God for giving us such a precious relic as his holy body, unworthy though we are of such a treasure. But we earnestly entreat you to think of us, and rely on our friendship, just as did the Blessed Giovanni; and as a special favour, although we do not deserve it, I beg that you will come and live with us." The venerable wife of the Blessed Giovanni thanked the Abbess and all the sisters, and then she and her relations sorrowfully took their departure. After that, everybody went away except the new father, Francesco Vincenti, and some of the poor brothers.

12*

CHAPTER LVI.

How the Blessed Francesco fell Sick seven days after the Death of the Blessed Giovanni.

FRANCESCO, who was staying with the chaplain of the convent, in his great grief wished for death, to reunite him to his beloved father in Christ, Giovanni; and he often said, with tears: " Oh, dear Giovanni, thou knowest how thou didst promise that I should only be parted from thee for a little while, and that after a few days I should rejoin thee. Thou hast never told me a lie; may God grant that *these* words may come true. Have pity on me, dear Giovanni, for although I am with my good companions, I feel very lonely without thee. When will the happy time come that I may see thee? Woe is me! for my banishment is prolonged." And in words like these he continually gave vent to his sorrow.

But the good God, who always listens to His

servants, willed to grant his holy desire; and as for
His sake he and the Blessed Giovanni had together
endured much worldly suffering, so it was His Will
that they should enjoy eternal happiness together,
and He visited Francesco with a great fever.   When
this good man felt it come upon him he was filled
with joy, and said, with S. John Baptist, "Blessed
art thou, O Lord, who hast remembered me."   His
sickness increased daily, but the brave Francesco
bore it very patiently, for he hoped that he should
die, and join his beloved Giovanni in eternal life.
And in his suffering he said: "Oh, Blessed Giovanni,
I see now that thou bearest me the same love in
death as thou didst in life, since God has heard thy
prayers on my behalf."

CHAPTER LVII.

How the Blessed Francesco died fifteen days after the
Death of the Blessed Giovanni.

AS his sickness increased, he demanded the
Holy Viaticum of Christ's Body, and when
Ser Ghero, Rector of the Church of S. Desiderio in
Siena, brought him the Most Holy Sacrament, Francesco humbly knelt before It; and after confessing
how ungrateful he had been for the blessings God
had granted him, and that he was the greatest
sinner in the world, he said some words in the same
form and manner as his father in Christ, the Blessed
Giovanni, had done, dictating them also to Benedetto
di Pace of the city of Castello.   This was on the 7th
of August in the same year, in the presence of
these his poor companions, who were cited as witnesses: Giovanni d'Ambrogio, Gualtieri di Piero, Giovanni di Messer Niccolo de Malescotti, Ambrogio di
Giucca, Matteo di Meglioruccio, Domenico di Guido,
and Bartoluccio di Santi of the town of Castello.

The Blessed Francesco was such a lover of holy poverty, that when he was very ill he laid on a mattress out in the street, and many people from Siena and other places visited him there, for he had a great many friends. His wonderful and holy life had gained him the friendship of many holy men, both secular and religious, who, moved by their love towards him, exhorted him to patience; unnecessarily so, however, for he exhorted them much more earnestly to despise temporal things, and long for the blessings of eternity, and they left him, very much edified by his fervent words.

One day, some of the family of the Piccoluomini came to see him, and as is the custom of many when they visit sick people, they comforted him, saying: "By God's mercy, thou wilt be cured, and be well and happy again; trust in the Lord;" and other such expressions. "My brothers," said the good Francesco, "you do not know God's secret thoughts. I would rather not recover, if that were His Will, for I am longing to go to Giovanni, my dear father, companion, and brother. I do not deserve it, because of my sins, but I hope for his merits God will count me worthy." They talked together a little longer, and at last the men said to Francesco: "Before we depart, we pray thee to give us some words of counsel;" but he answered them kindly, saying: "That is not for me, yet love constrains me just to say one word, and note it well—We must not let a good opportunity pass." And considering this saying, they left him, very much edified.

By his wonderful patience in this sickness, and his holy doctrine, Francesco taught every one who saw him, especially his sorrowing companions, who were utterly overwhelmed with grief. At last, about fifteen days after the death of his holy father, he received the last Sacraments with the greatest devotion, and in the presence of his sons in Christ yielded up his soul to God. His poor companions having lost the bodily presence of the supporters, or rather founders of their holy confraternity, renewed their weeping; but though their hearts were full of sorrow, they trusted in Jesus Christ, and in the merits and prayers of their blessed fathers, Giovanni and Francesco. And being joined by many sorrowing relations and friends, they sang the solemn Office of the Dead over the body of Francesco, and buried him by the side of his father in Christ, Giovanni.

From the time that these two soldiers of Christ gave up the world, till the day of their death, they

continued to grow in holiness, and with affectionate
solicitude sought after God's glory and the salvation of souls ; and thus sowing the Word of God by
their holy life and doctrine, thousands of persons
were turned to repentance. It seems to me that
Isaias prophesied of these two fathers, and of the
other poor ones of Jesus Christ, who for the glory of
God endured hunger, thirst, and many other hard-
ships, when he said, in the fourteenth chapter, "And
the first-born of the poor shall be fed, and the poor
shall rest with confidence;" for now in Paradise they
feed on heavenly food, and their poor brothers are
enjoying eternal rest with them.

CHAPTER LVIII.

A brief Description of the Person of the Blessed Giovanni, and of his Wisdom.

THE Blessed Giovanni was of a fair complexion, and small and delicately made, but the Blessed Francesco was strong and tall. The Blessed Giovanni never learnt grammar, or any other science, having from his boyhood been occupied in mercantile affairs; but owing to the virtues he practised after his conversion, and his continual meditation and prayer, he was greatly endued with learning, as his beautiful letters, burning with Divine wisdom, plainly show; and his charity was so great, that he would willingly have been put to death a hundred times a day, if he could have saved any souls thereby. His heart was literally on fire with Divine love, for which cause he always wore his coat unbuttoned, showing his naked flesh; and when speaking of the things of God, it seemed as if he

could hardly contain himself, so very earnest was
he. The Name of Christ was so impressed upon
his heart, that he often mentioned it; and in one
hundred of his letters which I have read, most of
them very short, I have found this name Christ
written about 1,400 times, without the other name
which is generally joined to it. Truly his conversation was in heaven, and his love to God was so
great, that he was almost consumed by it, like the
Blessed Giacopone da Todi.

Now it happened a few days after the Blessed
Giovanni had departed to the Lord, that the priest
Giovanni di Schiavo, mentioned a few pages back,
wrote to the Abbess of the Convent of Santa Bonda,
telling her how the Blessed Giovanni had revealed
to him in secret many things that were to happen,
which he was to make known to her only; so he
said he would come and see her, and tell her everything by word of mouth. But it pleased God after
this to take the priest's life, and so he did not go
there, and the things were never revealed.

CHAPTER LIX.

*Of some Miracles, which, by the grace of God, were
performed by the Blessed Giovanni after his death.*

NOW it happened not long after the death of
the Blessed Giovanni, that the devil (for what
cause I know not) entered into a young woman who
lived near the convent, and tormented her greatly.
One day she fled out of her house, and her parents
followed her to bring her back. But she went on till
at last she reached the convent, and as God willed it,
she found the church door open, so she went in, and
as she passed over the grave of the Blessed Giovanni
she suddenly fell down in a swoon. When her parents
came up to her they began to rub her with good wine,
and by the grace of the merciful God, when she came
to herself, she was perfectly cured, and entirely freed
from the evil spirit. When her parents asked how
it was that she had been so suddenly cured, she said
that when she stepped upon the saint's grave the

devil fled away, and she declared that it was the saint who was buried there who had delivered her from that evil spirit; and so they took her home, healed and set free, praising and thanking God and the Blessed Giovanni, and the young woman told everybody who asked her about it of the mercy she had miraculously received. This miracle was published throughout the city and province of Siena, and this being the case, the sisters, inspired by God, with great solemnity, and in the presence of many priests, caused that holy body to be disinterred, in order to remove it to a place more worthy of it. On opening the coffin, they found that all the flowers and sweet-smelling herbs with which his poor brothers had covered him were turned into mud and water, but the precious body was whole and sound, as if it had been only just buried. They removed him with great solemnity and devotion inside the church of this convent, inhabited by nuns only, and here they put him into a beautiful coffin which his venerable wife had had made for him, on which was painted the figure of our Lord Jesus Christ, also those of the Blessed Giovanni and Francesco; and this was seventeen months after his holy death. Here he was held in such great veneration, that many people devoutly came to see him.

God was graciously pleased to work another miracle
in one of the lay sisters of the convent. She was
afflicted with a sore disease in the thumb of her right
hand, which the doctors had for a long time tried to
cure ; but as she grew worse instead of better, and the
thumb had begun to mortify, they decided on taking
it off, to prevent the mortification spreading over the
hand. On hearing this the sister had recourse to
prayer, with much faith, humility, and contrition for
her sins, devoutly praying God, that by the merits of
the Blessed Giovanni, He would restore her to health,
so that she might not lose her thumb. She also
affectionately and reverently prayed the Blessed Giovanni to intercede with God for the healing of her
sore; and having passed the whole night in prayer,
when the morning came, she, full of faith, unfastened
the bandage round her hand, and found her thumb
was healed, and as sound as the other fingers, except
that it had no nail. When she saw this miracle she
heartily thanked God and the Blessed Giovanni, and
again had recourse to earnest and faithful prayer to
God and the Blessed Giovanni, that the nail might
be restored, which prayer God in His mercy granted,
seeing her pure faith. All the sisters, greatly mar-
velling at this miracle, returned thanks to God, and

when the doctors came and found the diseased finger whole as the others, they also, greatly wondering at this sign, thanked God, and published it throughout Siena, and many people went to the convent and certified themselves of the miracle.

The holy body of the Blessed Giovanni being thus honourably and reverently kept in the coffin above mentioned, many people devoutly came to see it; and when, in time of war, the sisters for greater safety went to stay at Siena, they always had it taken to that monastery. But afterwards, to prevent the necessity of removing it in time of war, they caused a secret vault to be built in the church, in which they kept it, and here it remained whole and sound for twenty years. But as the devotion and frequent visits of the people increased, the chaplain of the convent, Giovanni d'Ambrogio, who has often been mentioned before, fearing that the coming and going of so many people might in future distract the minds of the sisters, or for some other reason, once, when they were gone to Siena in time of war, arranged, so report says, that the water from a pipe in the roof should secretly drop upon the vault, so as to corrupt that holy body, hoping that when the flesh was wasted away such a multitude would not come to see it. And so the sisters found it all corrupted except one foot, which remains entire and without blemish to this day. The venerable wife of the Blessed Giovanni lived some years after his death. She practised much self-mortification, and spent most of her time in her private oratory, praying, or reading some religious book, of which she had many. She was very charitable, and often gave away food to the poor, especially to the poor Gesuati, who when they came to Siena lodged at her house, as they did when the Blessed Giovanni was living; and in the year 1371 she made her will, and desired that she might be buried as a nun in the Convent of Santa Bonda. Soon after this she yielded up her soul to God, and was buried in the convent with much honour and devotion.

Now it happened while the venerable and holy Paola was Abbess of Santa Bonda, that a woman called Nutina, who was possessed of the devil, was taken to the holy body of the Blessed Giovanni, and the Abbess and other devout sisters sought by psalms, prayers, and other words, to force the evil spirit to depart from her. At last the Abbess said to it: "I command thee, by the power of Jesus Christ, and the merits of the Blessed Giovanni, to come out of this woman, and to give us some sign that thou hast departed." The devil replied, " What sign wilt thou have?" " Go into that lamp which is before the altar," said the Abbess. " I cannot go there," he said, " for I am not worthy." The Abbess answered, " Do as thou wilt, only give us some sign of thy departure." Then the woman was delivered from the unclean spirit, and in a wine cellar of the convent, where there was a well of water, there came such a smell of sulphur, that for three weeks the sisters were unable to enter it.

There was a very devout and self-denying lady, the wife of Messer Martino di Simone, a citizen of Siena, and during the pestilence of the year 1400, she gave away to the sick poor so much of a very good wine which they possessed, that a cask was emptied only a few days after it had been tapped. Upon this she began to weep bitterly for fear of her husband, who was a very hard, severe man ; and in her necessity she prayed most earnestly and humbly to the Blessed Giovanni, that he would free her from this trouble. As soon as she had finished her prayer she found the cask was full, so that even Messer Martino wondered afterwards that it was so long in emptying.

A venerable citizen of Siena, called Marco Ciotti,

who had no children, prayed to the Blessed Giovanni, and immediately afterwards his wife conceived, and a son was born to him, whom he called Giacopo; and after this another, and he was called Rinaldo.

In the month of July, A.D. 1435, a poor woman, Francesco di Meo dello Scassa, being possessed with a devil, was taken to the body of the Blessed Giovanni, and by his merits she was, in the presence of the sisters, delivered from the evil spirit.

Cecco di Buonaventura Colombini, an honoured citizen of Siena, having no sons, devoutly prayed to the Blessed Giovanni, and promised, that if God gave him a son, he would make him, as far as lay in his power, one of the poor Gesuati. After this vow his wife conceived, and bore him a son. He called him Giovampiero, and clothed him in the habit of the Gesuati.

Here ends the holy life of the Blessed Giovanni di Piero di Jacopo Colombini, written by Feo di Feo di Jacopo Belcari, a citizen of Florence, A.D. 1448.

In omnibus glorificetur Deus.

R. WASHBOURNE, PRINTER, 18 PATERNOSTER ROW, LONDON.

Oratorian Lives of the Saints.

SECOND SERIES.

1. It is proposed to publish a Second Series of the Lives
of the Modern Saints, translated from foreign languages, and
to bring out two or more volumes in the year.

2. The works translated from will be in most cases the Lives
drawn up *for* or *from* the processes of canonisation or beatification, as being more full, more authentic, and more replete
with anecdote, thus enabling the reader to become better
acquainted with the Saint's disposition and spirit; while the
simple matter-of-fact style of the narrative is, from its unobtrusive character, more adapted for spiritual reading than
the views, and generalisations, and apologetic extenuations
of more recent biographers.

3. The objects are those stated at the commencement of the
First Series: viz., 1. To supply English Catholics with a
cabinet-library of interesting as well as edifying reading,
especially for families, schools, and religious refectories, which
would for many reasons be particularly adapted for these times,
and would, with God's blessing, act as a counter-influence to
the necessarily deadening and chilling effects which the neighbourhood of heresy and the consequent prevalence of earthly
principles and low views of grace may have on the temper and
habits of mind even of the faithful: 2. To present to our
other countrymen a number of samples of the fruit which the
system, doctrine, and moral discipline established by the holy
and blessed Council of Trent have produced, and which will be,

to inquirers really in earnest about their souls, an argument more cogent than any that mere controversy can allege : and 3. To spread the honour and love of the ever-blessed Queen of Saints, by showing how greatly an intense devotion to her aided in forming those prodigies of heroic virtue with which the Holy Ghost has been pleased to adorn the Church since the schism of Luther, *more than in almost any previous times ;* while the same motive will prevent the Series being confined to modern saints *exclusively.*

4. The work is published with the permission and approval of superiors. Every volume containing the Life of a person not yet canonised or beatified by the Church will be prefaced by a protest in conformity with the decree of Urban VIII., and in all Lives which introduce questions of mystical theology great care will be taken to publish nothing which has not had adequate sanction, or without the reader being informed of the nature and amount of the sanction.

———

R. WASHBOURNE'S CATALOGUE.

JULY 1874.

New Books.

Stories of the Saints for Children. By M. F. S., author of " Tom's Crucifix, and other Tales," " Catherine Hamilton," &c. Fcap. 8vo. 3s. 6d.

Oratorian Lives of the Saints. 2nd Series. *See page* 18. S. Veronica Giuliani, and B. Battista Varani. 5s.

Sketch of the Life and Letters of the Countess Adelstan. An abridged translation from the Frenoh of the Rev. Père Marquigny, S.J., by E. A. M., author of " Rosalie, or the Memoirs of a French Child," " Life of Paul Seigneret, &c." 2s. 6d.

Life of B. Giovanni Colombini. By Feo Belcari. Translated from the editions of 1541 and 1832. Cr. 8vo. 3s. 6d.

On Contemporary ¦Prophecies. By Mgr. Dupanloup. Translated, by permission of the Bishop of Orleans, by Rev. Dr. Redmond. 8vo. 1s.

Photographs. A set of 10, illustrating the history of the Miraculous Hosts, called the Blessed Sacrament of the Miracle. Bruxelles, A.D. 1370. Price 2s. 6d. the set.

First Communion Picture. Tastefully printed in gold and colours. Price 1s., or 10s. a dozen, *net.*

"Just what has long been wanted, a really good picture, with Tablet for First Communion and Confirmation."—*Tablet.*

₌ *Though this Catalogue does not contain the books of other Publishers, R. W. can supply all of them, no matter by whom they are published.*

R. Washbourne, 18 Paternoster Row, London.

The Supernatural Life.   Translated from the French of Mgr. Mermillod, with a Preface by Lady Herbert.   Cr. 8vo. 5s.

" Among the Catholic prelates on the Continent, no name stands higher than that of Dr. Mermillod, the exiled Bishop of Geneva, whose eloquence struck so forcibly the English pilgrims at Paray-le-Monial last year. . . The object of these conferences was to stir up the female portion of creation to higher and holier lives, in the hope of so influencing their husbands, their brothers, and other relatives, and so to lend a helping hand to the right side in that struggle which, as Lady Herbert so eloquently and so truly remarks, 'was formerly confined to certain places and certain minds, but is now going on all over the world—the struggle between God and the devil ; between faith and unbelief ; between those who still revere the word of God, and the entire negation of all divine revelation.' "— *Register.*

The Jesuits, and other Essays.   By Willis Nevin.   Fcap. 8vo. 2s. 6d.

" If any one wishes to read in brief all that can be said about and in favour of the sons of Ignatius Loyola, by all means let him get this little work, where he will find everything ready ' at his fingers' ends.' "— *Register.*   " They are in the rough but earnest style, and perhaps are not the worse for being decidedly plain.   Altogether, a Protestant, inclined to make rash statements upon Catholic subjects, will find these tracts a very awkward stumbling block in the pathway of his silliness."—*Universe.*   " It displays considerable vigour of thought, and no small literary power.   This small book is a work of promise from one who knows both sides of those questions."— *Union Review.*

The Village Lily.   Fcap. 8vo. 1s. ; gilt, 1s. 6d.

Sermons, Lectures, &c.   By Rev. M. B. Buckley.   6s.

Devotions to the Sacred Heart.   By the Rev. J. Joy Dean.   Fcap. 8vo. 3s.

The Life of Pleasure.   Translated from the French of Mgr. Dechamps.   Fcap. 8vo. 1s. 6d.

Catherine Hamilton.   By the author of "Tom's Crucifix," "Stories of the Saints for Children," &c.   Fcap. 8vo. 2s. 6d. ; gilt, 3s.

" A short, simple, and well-told story, illustrative of the power of grace to correct bad temper in a wayward girl.   For Catholic parents who are possessed with such children, we know of no better book than ' Catherine Hamilton.' "—*Register.*   " We have no doubt this will prove a very attractive book to the little folks, and would be glad to see it widely circulated."—*American Catholic World.*

R. Washbourne, 18 *Paternoster Row, London.*

Novena of Meditations in Honour of S. Joseph, according to the method of S. Ignatius; preceded by a new exercise for hearing Mass according to the intentions of the souls in Purgatory. 18mo. 1s. 6d.

Instructions for the Sacrament of Confirmation. 6d.

Düsseldorf Society for the Distribution of Good, Religious Pictures. R. Washbourne is now Sole Agent for Great Britain and Ireland. Yearly Subscription is 8s. 6d. *Catalogue post free.*

Düsseldorf Gallery. 8vo. half morocco, 31s. 6d. This volume contains 127 Engravings handsomely bound in half morocco, full gilt. Cash 25s.

Düsseldorf Gallery. 4to. half morocco, £6. This superb work contains 331 Pictures. Handsomely bound in half morocco, full gilt. Cash £5.

"We confidently believe that no wealthy Catholic could possibly see the volume which we have examined and admired without ordering 'The Düsseldorf Gallery' for the adornment of his drawing-room table. . . As lovers of art, we rejoice to see what has been done, and we can only desire with all possible heartiness, that such an enterprise as this may meet with the success it deserves."—*Tablet.* "The most beautiful Catholic gift-book that was ever sent forth from the house of a Catholic publisher."—*Register.*

Dramas, Comedies, Farces.

He would be a Lord. From the French of "Le Bourgeois Gentilhomme." Three Acts. (Boys.) 2s.

St. Louis in Chains. Drama in Five Acts, for boys. 2s.
"Well suited for acting in Catholic schools and colleges."—*Tablet.*

The Expiation. A Drama in Three Acts, for boys. 2s.
"Has its scenes laid in the days of the Crusades."—*Register.*

Shandy Maguire. A Farce for boys in Two Acts. 1s.

The Reverse of the Medal. A Drama in Four Acts, for young ladies. 6d.

Ernscliff Hall: or, Two Days Spent with a Great-Aunt. A Drama in Three Acts, for young ladies. 6d.

Filiola. A Drama in Four Acts, for young ladies. 6d.

The Convent Martyr, or Callista. By Dr. Newman. Dramatized by Dr. Husenbeth. 1s.

Garden of the Soul. (WASHBOURNE'S EDITION.) *With Imprimatur of the Archbishop of Westminster*. This edition has over all others the following advantages :—1. Complete order in its arrangements. 2. Introduction of Devotions to Saint Joseph, Patron of the Church. 3. Introduction into the English Devotions for Mass to a very great extent of the Prayers from the Missal. 4. The full Form of Administration of all the Sacraments publicly administered in Church. 5. The insertion of Indulgences above Indulgenced Prayers. 6. Its large size of type. Embossed, 1s. ; with rims, 1s. 6d. ; with Epistles and Gospels, 1s. 6d.; with rims, 2s. French morocco, 2s. ; with rims, 2s. 6d. ; with E. and G., 2s. 6d. ; with rims, 3s. French morocco extra gilt, 2s. 6d. ; with rims, 3s.; with E. and G., 3s. ; with rims, 3s. 6d. Calf or morocco, 4s. ; with rims, 5s. 6d. ; with E. and G., 4s. 6d. ; with rims, 6s. Calf or morocco extra, 5s.; with rims, 6s. 6d. ; with E. and G., 5s. 6d. ; with rims, 7s. Velvet, with rims, 8s., 10s. 6d, and 13s. ; with E. and G., 8s. 6d., 11s., and 13s. 6d. Russia, antique, with clasp, 12s. 6d.; with E. and G., 13s. Ivory, 15s., 21s., 25s., and 30s.; with E. and G., 15s. 6d., 21s. 6d., 25s. 6d., and 30s. 6d. Antique bindings, with corners and clasps : morocco, 28s., with E. and G., 28s. 6d. ; russia, 30s., with E. and G., 30s. 6d.

The Epistles and Gospels in cloth, 6d., roan, 1s. 6d.

' This is one of the best editions we have seen of one of the best of all our Prayer-books. It is well printed in clear large type, on good paper."—*Catholic Opinion*. "A very complete arrangement of this which is emphatically the Prayer-book of every Catholic household. It is as cheap as it is good, and we heartily recommend it."—*Universe*. "Two striking features are the admirable order displayed throughout the book and the insertion of the Indulgences, in small type above Indulgenced Prayers."—*Weekly Register*.

The Little Garden. Cloth, 6d., with rims, 1s. ; em.

bossed, 9d., with rims, 1s. 3d. ; roan, 1s., with rims, 1s. 6d. ; french morocco, 1s. 6d., with rims, 2s. ; french morocco, extra gilt, 2s., with rims, 2s. 6d. ; imitation ivory, with rims, 3s. ; calf or morocco, 3s., with rims, 4s. ; calf or morocco, extra gilt, 4s., with rims, 5s. ; velvet, with rims, 5s., 8s. 6d., 10s. 6d. ; russia, with clasp, 8s. ; ivory, with rims, 10s. 6d., 13s., 15s., 17s. 6d. ; antique binding, with clasps : morocco, 17s. 6d., russia, 20s. ; with oxydized silver or gilt mountings, in morocco case, 30s.

A Few Words from Lady Mildred's Housekeeper. 2d.

"If any of our lady readers wish to give to their servants some hints as to the necessity of laying up some part of their wages instead of spending their money in dressing above their station, let them get 'A Few Words from Lady Mildred's Housekeeper,' and present it for the use of the servants' hall or downstairs department. The good advice of an experienced upper servant on such subjects ought not to fall on unwilling ears."—*Register.* "A short tract of good advice to servant girls about dress."—*Tablet.*

Religious Reading.

"Vitis Mystica ;" or, the True Vine. A Treatise on the Passion of Our Lord. Translated, with Preface, by the Rev. W. R. Bernard Brownlow. With Frontispiece. 18mo. 4s., red edges, 4s. 6d.

"It is a pity that such a beautiful treatise should for so many centuries have remained untranslated into our tongue."—*Tablet.* "It will be found very acceptable spiritual food."—*Church Herald.* "We heartily recommend it for its unction and deep sense of the beauties of nature."—*The Month.* "Full of deep spiritual lore."—*Register.* "Every chapter of this little volume affords abundant matter for meditation."—*Universe.* "An excellent translation of a beautiful treatise."—*Dublin Review.*

Ebba ; or, the Supernatural Power of the Blessed Sacrament. In French. 12mo. 1s. 6d. ; cloth gilt, 2s. 6d.

"The author has caught very well many of the difficulties which bar the way to the Church in this country...We may venture to hope that the work will also bear fruit on the Continent."—*The Month.* "There are thoughts in the work which we value highly."—*Dublin Review.* "It is a clever and trenchant work. . . Written in a lively and piquant style."—*Register.* "The tone of the book is kind and fervent."—*Church Herald.* "The book is exceedingly well written, and will do good to all who read it."—*Universe.*

Holy Places ; their Sanctity and Authenticity. By the
Rev. Fr. Philpin. With Maps. Crown 8vo. 6s.

"It displays an amount of patient research not often to be met
with."—*Universe.* "Dean Stanley and other sinners in controversy
are treated with great gentleness. They are indeed thoroughly exposed and refuted."—*Register.* "Fr. Philpin has a particularly
nervous and fresh style of handling his subject, with an occasional
picturesqueness of epithet or simile."—*Tablet.* "We do not question
his learning and industry, and yet we cannot think them to have
been uselessly expended on this work."—*Spectator.* ". . . Fr.
Philpin there weighs the comparative value of extraordinary, ordinary, and natural evidence, and gives an admirable summary of the
witness of the early centuries regarding the holy places of Jerusalem,
with archæological and architectural proofs. It is a complete treatise of the subject."—*The Month.* "The author treats his subject
with a thorough system, and a competent knowledge. It is a book
of singular attractiveness and considerable merit."—*Church Herald.*
"Fr. Philpin's very interesting book appears most opportunely, and
at a time when pilgrimages have been revived."—*Dublin Review.*

The Consoler ; or, Pious Readings addressed to the
Sick and to all who are afflicted. By the Rev.
P. J. Lambilotte, S.J. Translated by the Right
Rev. Abbot Burder, O. Cist. Fcp. 8vo. 4s. 6d.,
red edges, 5s.

"As 'The Consoler' has the merit of being written in plain and
simple language, and while deeply spiritual contains no higher
flights into the regions ol : mysticism where poor and ignorant
readers would be unable to follow, it is very specially adapted for
one of the subjects which its writer had in view,—namely, its introduction into hospitals."—*Tablet.* "A work replete with wise
comfort for every affliction."—*Universe.* "A spiritual treatise of
great beauty and value."—*Church Herald.*

Flowers of Christian Wisdom. By Lucien Henry.
With a Preface by the Right Hon. Lady Herbert
of Lea. 18mo. 2s. ; red edges, 2s. 6d.

"A compilation of some of the most beautiful thoughts and
passages in the works of the Fathers, the great schoolmen, and
eminent modern Churchmen, and will probably secure a good cir-
culation."—*Church Times.* "It is a compilation of gems of thought,
carefully selected."—*Tablet.* "It is a small but exquisite bou-
quet, like that which S. Francis of Sales has prepared for *Philothea.*"
—*Universe.*

The Souls in Purgatory. Translated from the French,
by the Right Rev. Abbot Burder, O. Cist. 32mo. 3d.

"It will be found most useful as an aid to the cultivation of this
especial devotion."—*Register.*

The Happiness of Heaven. By a Father of the Society of Jesus. Fcap. 8vo. 4s.

God our Father. By the same Author. Fcap. 8vo. 4s.

"Both of these books we can highly recommend."—*Register.*

The Light of the Holy Spirit in the World. By the Rev. Canon Hedley, O.S.B. 1s.; cloth, 1s. 6d.

A General History of the Catholic Church : from the commencement of the Christian Era until the present time. By the Abbé Darras. 4 vols., large 8vo. cloth, 48s.

The Book of Perpetual Adoration ; or, the Love of Jesus in the most Holy Sacrament of the Altar. By Mgr. Boudon. Edited by the Rev. J. Redman, D.D. Fcap. 8vo. 3s. ; red edges, 3s. 6d.

"This new translation is one of Boudon's most beautiful works, . . . and merits that welcome in no ordinary degree."—*Tablet.* "The devotions at the end will be very acceptable aids in visiting the Blessed Sacrament, and there are two excellent methods for assisting at Mass."—*The Month.* "It has been pronounced by a learned and pious French priest to be 'the most beautiful of all books' written in honour of the Blessed Sacrament." —*The Nation.*

Spiritual Works of Louis of Blois, Abbot of Liesse. Edited by the Rev. John Edward Bowden, of the Oratory. Fcap. 8vo. 3s. 6d ; red edges, 4s.

"No more important or welcome addition could have been made to our English ascetical literature than this little book. It is a model of good translation."—*Dublin Review.* "This handy little volume will certainly become a favourite."—*Tablet.* "Elegant and flowing."—*Register.* "Most useful of meditations."—*Catholic Opinion.*

Heaven Opened by the Practice of Frequent Confession and Communion. By the Abbé Favre. Translated from the French, carefully revised by a Father of the Society of Jesus. Third Edition. Fcap. 8vo. 3s. 6d. ; red edges, 4s. Cheap edit. 2s.

"This beautiful little book of devotion. We may recommend it to the clergy as well as to the laity."—*Tablet.* "It is filled with quotations from the Holy Scriptures, the Fathers, and the Councils of the Church, and thus will be found of material assistance to the clergy, as a storehouse of doctrinal and ascetical authorities on the two great sacraments of Holy Eucharist and Penance."—*Register.*

The Spiritual Life. — Conferences delivered to the *Enfants de Marie* by Père Ravignan. Cr. 8vo. 5s.

" Père Ravignan's words are as applicable to the ladies of London as to those of Paris. They could not have a better book for their spiritual reading."—*Tablet.* " These discourses appear to be admirably suited to English Catholics at the present moment."—*Westminster Gazette.* " A depth of eloquence and power of exhortation which few living preachers can rival."—*Church Review.*

Lenten Thoughts. Drawn from the Gospel for each day in Lent. By the Bishop of Northampton. 1s. 6d. ; stronger bound, 2s. ; red edges, 2s. 6d.

" A beautiful little volume of Meditations."—*Universe.* " Will be found a useful manual."—*Tablet.* " An admirable little book." —*Nation.* " Clear and practical."—*The Month.* " A very beautiful and simple little book."—*Church Herald.*

Contemplations on the Most Holy Sacrament of the Altar, drawn from the Sacred Scriptures. 18mo. cloth, 2s. ; cloth extra, red edges, 2s. 6d.

" This is a welcome addition to our books of Scriptural devotion. It contains thirty-four excellent subjects of reflection before the Blessed Sacrament, or for making a spiritual visit to the Blessed Sacrament at home ; for the use of the sick."—*Dublin Review.*

One Hundred Pious Reflections. Extracted from Alban Butler's "Lives of the Saints." 18mo. cloth, red edges, 2s. ; cheap edition, 1s.

" A happy idea. The author of ' The Lives of the Saints ' had a way of breathing into his language the unction and force which carries the truth of the Gospel into the heart."—*Letter to the Editor from* THE RIGHT REV. DR. ULLATHORNE, BISHOP OF BIRMINGHAM. " Well selected, sufficiently short, and printed in good bold type."—*Tablet.* " Good, sound practical reflections."—*Church Herald.*

The Imitation of Christ. With reflections. 32mo. 1s. Persian calf, 3s. 6d. Also an Edition with ornamental borders. Fcap. cloth, red edges, 3s. 6d.

Following of Christ. Small pocket edition, with initial letters. 1s. ; embossed red edges, 1s. 6d. ; roan, 2s ; French morocco, 2s. 6d. ; calf or morocco, 4s. 6d. ; calf or morocco extra gilt, 5s. 6d. ; ivory, 15s. and 16s. ; morocco antique, 17s. 6d. ; russia antique, 20s.

Conversion of the Teutonic Race. By Mrs. Hope, author of " Early Martyrs." Edited by the Rev. Father Dalgairns. 2 vols. crown 8vo. 12s.

I. Conversion of the Franks and the English, 6s.
II. S. Boniface and the Conversion of Germany, 6s.

" It is good in itself, possessing considerable literary merit ; is forms one of the few Catholic books brought out in this country which are not translations or adaptations."—*Dublin Review.* " It is a great thing to find a writer of a book of this class so clearly grasping, and so boldly setting forth truths, which, familiar as they are to scholars, are still utterly unknown by most of the writers of our smaller literature."—*Saturday Review.* "A very valuable work . . . . Mrs. Hope has compiled an original history, which gives constant evidence of great erudition, and sound historical judgment."—*Month.* "This is a most taking book : it is solid history and romance in one."—*Catholic Opinion.* " It is carefully, and in many parts beautifully written."—*Universe.*

Cistercian Order : its Mission and Spirit. Comprising the Life of S. Robert of Newminster, and the Life of S. Robert of Knaresborough. By the author of " Cistercian Legends." Crown 8vo. 3s. 6d.

Cistercian Legends of the 13th Century. Translated from the Latin by the Rev. Henry Collins. 3s.

" Interesting records of Cistercian sanctity and cloistral experience."—*Dublin Review.* " A casquet of jewels. ."—*Weekly Register.* " Most beautiful legends, full of deep spiritual reading."—*Tablet.* " Well translated, and beautifully got up."—*Month.* "A compilation of anecdotes, full of heavenly wisdom."—*Catholic Opinion.*

The Directorium Asceticum ; or, Guide to the Spiritual Life. By Scaramelli. Translated and Edited at St. Beuno's College. 4 vols. crown 8vo. 24s.

Maxims of the Kingdom of Heaven. New and enlarged Edition. 5s. ; red edges, 5s. 6d. ; calf or morocco, 10s. 6d.

" The selections on every subject are numerous, and the order and arrangement of the chapters will greatly facilitate meditation and reference."—*Freeman's Journal.* " We are glad to see that this admirable devotional work, of which we have before spoken in warm praise, has reached a second issue."—*Weekly Register.* " It has an Introduction by J. H. N., and bears the Imprimatur of the Archbishop of Westminster. We need say no more in its praise."—*Tablet.* " A most beautiful little book."—*Catholic Opinion.* "This priceless volume."—*Universe.* " Most suitable for meditation and reference."—*Dublin Review.*

R. Washbourne, 18 *Paternoster Row, London.*

The Oxford Undergraduate of Twenty Years Ago:
his Religion, his Studies, his Antics. By a
Bachelor of Arts. [Author of "The Comedy of
Convocation."] 2s. 6d. ; cloth, 3s. 6d.

" The writing is full of brilliancy and point."—*Tablet.* "Time
has not dimmed the author's recollection, and has no doubt served
to sharpen his sense of undergraduate humour and his reading of
undergraduate character."—*Examiner.* " It will deservedly attract
attention, not only by the briskness and liveliness of its style, but
also by the accuracy of the picture which it probably gives of an
individual experience."—*The Month.* " Whoever takes this book
in hand will read it through and through with the keenest pleasure
and with great benefit."—*Universe.*

The Infallibility of the Pope. A Lecture. By the
Author of " The Oxford Undergraduate," " Comedy of Convocation," &c. 8vo. 1s.

"A splendid lecture, by one who thoroughly understands his
subject, and in addition is possessed of a rare power of language in
which to put before others what he himself knows so well."—*Universe.* " There are few writers so well able to make things plain
and intelligible as the author of 'The Comedy of Convocation.'. . .
The lecture is a model of argument and style."—*Register.*

Comedy of Convocation in the English Church.
Edited by Archdeacon Chasuble, D.D. 2s. 6d.

" Give me leave to be merry on a merry subject."—*S. Greg. Naz.*

The Harmony of Anglicanism. Report of a Con-
ference on Church Defence. [By T. W. M. Mar-
shall, Esq.] 8vo. 2s. 6d.

." 'Church Defence' is characterized by the same caustic irony,
the same good-natured satire, the same logical acuteness which distinguished its predecessor, the 'Comedy of Convocation.' . . . A
more scathing bit of irony we have seldom met with."—*Tablet.*
" Clever, humorous, witty, learned, written by a keen but sarcastic
observer of the Establishment, it is calculated to make defenders
wince as much as it is to make all others smile."—*Nonconformist.*

Consoling Thoughts of St. Francis de Sales. By Père
Huguet. 18mo., 2s.

Holy Readings. Short Selections from well-known
Authors. By J. R. Digby Beste, Esq. 32mo.
cloth, 2s. ; cloth, red edges, 2s. 6d. ; roan, 3s. ;
morocco, 6s. [See "Catholic Hours," p. 23.]

Benedictine Almanack. Yearly. Price 1d.

St. Peter; his Name and his Office as set forth in Holy Scripture. By T. W. Allies. *Second Edition.* Revised. Crown 8vo. 5s.

" A standard work. There is no single book in English, on the Catholic side, which contains the Scriptural argument about St. Peter and the Papacy so clearly or conclusively put."—*Month.* " An admirable volume."—*The Universe.* " This valuable work." —*Weekly Register.* " A second edition, with a new and very touching preface."—*Dublin Review.*

Complete Works of Saint John of the Cross. 2 vols, 8vo. 28s.

The Roman Question. By Dr. Husenbeth. 1s.

The Knight of the Faith. By the Rev. Dr. Laing.

1. A Favourite Fallacy about Private Judgment and Inquiry. 1d.
2. Catholic not Roman Catholic. 4d.
3. Rationale of the Mass. 1s.
4. Challenge to the Churches of England, Scotland, and all Protestant Denominations. 1d.
5. Absurd Protestant Opinions concerning *Intention*, and Spelling Book of Christian Philosophy. 4d.
6. Whence the Monarch's right to rule. 2s. 6d.
7. Protestantism against the Natural Moral Law. 1d.
8. What is Christianity? 6d.

Catholic Calendar and Guide to the Services of the Church. Yearly. Price 6d.

Dr. Pusey's Eirenicon considered in Relation to Catholic Unity. By H. N. Oxenham. 2s. 6d.

Sancti Alphonsi Doctoris Officium Parvum—Novena and Little Office in honour of St. Alphonsus. Fcap. 8vo. 1s.; cloth, 2s.; cloth extra, 3s.

Synodi Dioeceseos Suthwarcensis ad ejusdem erectione anno 1850 ad finem anni 1868 habitæ. 8vo. cloth, 7s. 6d.; 1869-70, 1s.

Sweetness of Holy Living; or Honey culled from the Flower Garden of S. Francis of Sales. 1s.; French morocco, 3s.

" In it will be found some excellent aids to devotion and meditation."—*Weekly Register.*

Men and Women of the English Reformation, from the days of Wolsey to the death of Cranmer. By S. H. Burke, M.A. 2 vols. 13s. Vol. ii., 6s. 6d.

"It contains a great amount of curious and useful information, gathered together with evident care."—*Dublin Review.* "Interesting and valuable."—*Tablet.* "It is, in truth, the only dispassionate record of a much contested epoch we have ever read."—*Cosmopolitan.* "It is so forcibly, but truthfully written, that it should be in the hands of every seeker after truth."—*Catholic Opinion.*—"On all hands admitted to be one of the most valuable historical works ever published."—*Nation.* "The author produces evidence that cannot be gainsayed."—*Universe.* "Full of interest, and very temperately written."—*Church Review.* "Able, fairly impartial, and likely to be of considerable value to the student of history. Replete with information."—*Church Times.* "The book supplies many hitherto unknown facts of the times of which it is a history."—*Church Opinion.* "A clever and well-written historical statement of facts concerning the chief actors of our so-called Reformation."—*The Month.*

Père Lacordaire's Conferences. God, 6s. Jesus Christ, 6s. God and Man, 6s.

A Devout Paraphrase on the Seven Penitential Psalms; or, a Practical Guide to Repentance. By the Rev. Fr. Blyth. To which is added:—Necessity of Purifying the Soul, by St. Francis of Sales. 18mo., 1s. 6d.; red edges, 2s.; cheap edition, 1s.

"A new edition of a book well known to our grandfathers. The work is full of devotion and of the spirit of prayer."—*Universe.* "A very excellent work, and ought to be in the hands of every Catholic."—*Waterford News.*

A New Miracle at Rome; through the Intercession of Blessed John Berchmans. 2d.

Cure of Blindness; through the Intercession of Our Lady and St. Ignatius. 2d.

Diary of a Confessor of the Faith. 12mo. 1s.

BY THE POOR CLARES OF KENMARE.

Book of the Blessed Ones. 4s. 6d.
A Nun's Advice to her Girls. 2s. 6d.
Daily Steps to Heaven. Fcap. 8vo. 4s. 6d.
Jesus and Jerusalem; or, the Way Home. 4s. 6d.
The Spouse of Christ. Crown 8vo. 7s. 6d.
The Ecclesiastical Year. Fcap. 4s. 6d.; calf, 6s. 6d.

A Homely Discourse ; Mary Magdalen.   Cr. 8vo. 6d.
Extemporaneous Speaking.   By Rev. T. J. Potter.   5s.
Pastor and People.   By Rev. T. J. Potter.   6s.
Meditations on the Veni Sancte Spiritus.   1s.
Eight Short Sermon Essays.   By Dr.'Redmond.   1s.
Non Possumus ; or, the Temporal Sovereignty of the
     Popes.   By the Rev. Father Lockhart.   1s.
Secession or Schism.   By Fr. Lockhart.   6d.
Who is the Anti-Christ of Prophecy?   By the Rev.
     Fr. Lockhart.   1s.
The Communion of Saints.   By the Rev. Father
     Lockhart.   1s. ; cloth, 1s. 6d.
The Church of England and its Defenders.   By the
     Rev. W. R. Bernard Brownlow.   8vo.   1st Letter,
     6d. ; 2nd Letter, 1s.
Lectures on the Life, Writings, and Times of Edmund
     Burke.   By Professor Robertson.   Crown 8vo.
     cloth, 5s.
Professor Robertson's Lectures on Modern History
     and Biography.   Crown 8vo. cloth, 6s.
Sursum, 1s.   Homeward, 2s.   Both by Rev. Fr. Rawes.
Sermon at the Month's Mind of the Most Rev. Dr.
     Spalding, Archbishop of Baltimore.   1s.
Monastic Legends.   By E. G. K. Browne.   8vo. 6d.

BY DR. MANNING, ARCHBISHOP OF WESTMINSTER.

The Convocation in Crown and Council.   6d. net.
Confidence in God.   Fcap. 1s. ; cloth, 1s. 6d.
Temporal Sovereignty of the Popes.   1s. ; cloth, 1s. 6d.
The Church, the Spirit, and the Word.   6d.

BY THE PASSIONIST FATHERS.

The School of Jesus Crucified.   3s. 6d. ; morocco, 5s.
The Manual of the Cross and Passion.   32mo. 2s. 6d.
The Manual of the Seven Dolours.   32mo.   1s. 6d.
The Christian Armed.   32mo.   1s. 6d. ; mor. 3s. 6d.
Guide to Sacred Eloquence.   2s.

Religious Instruction.

The Catechism of Christian Doctrine. Approved for the use of the Faithful in all the Dioceses of England and Wales. Price 1d. ; cloth, 2d.

The Catechism, Illustrated with Passages from the Holy Scriptures. Arranged by the Rev. J. B. Bagshawe, with Imprimatur. Crown 8vo. 2s. 6d.

"I believe the Catechism to be one of the best possible books of controversy, to those, at least, who are inquiring with a real desire to find the truth."—*Extract from the Preface.*

"An excellent idea. The very thing of all others that is needed by many under instruction."—*Tablet.* "It is a book which will do incalculable good. Our priests will hail with pleasure so valuable a help to their weekly instructions in the Catechism, while in schools its value will be equally recognized."— *Weekly Register.* "A work of great merit."—*Church Herald.* "We can hardly wish for anything better, either in intention or in performance."—*The Month.* "Very valuable."—*Dublin Review.*

A Dogmatic Catechism. By Frassinetti. Translated from the original Italian by the Oblate Fathers of St. Charles. With a Preface by His Grace the Archbishop of Westminster. Fcap. 8vo. 3s.

"We give a few extracts from Frassinetti's work, as samples of its excellent execution."—*Dublin Review.* "Needs no commendation."—*Month.* "It will be found useful, not only to catechists, but also for the instruction of converts from the middle class of society."—*Tablet.*

A First Sequel to the Catechism. By the Rev. J. Nary. 32mo. 1d.

"It will recommend itself to teachers in Catholic schools as one peculiarly adapted to the use of such children as have mastered the Catechism, and yet have nothing else to fall back upon for higher religious instruction. It will be found a great assistance as well to teachers as to pupils who belong to the higher standards in our Catholic poor schools."—*Weekly Register.*

Catechism made Easy. A Familiar Explanation of "The Catechism of Christian Doctrine." By the Rev. H. Gibson. Fcap. 8vo. Vol. I., 4s. 6d. Vol II., 4s. 6d.

The Monitor of the Association of Prayer. Monthly, 1d. Volume, 2s. Notices, 6s. 1000. Prints, 7s. 6d. 1000. Zelator's Cards, 10s. 1000.

R. Washbourne, 18 *Paternoster Row, London.*

The Threshold of the Catholic Church. A course of Plain Instructions for those entering her Communion. By Rev. J. B. Bagshawe. Cr. 8vo. 4s.

"A scholarly, well-written book, full of information."—*Church Herald.* "An admirable book, which will be of infinite service to thousands."—*Universe.* "Plain, practical, and unpretentious, it exhausts so entirely the various subjects of instruction necessary for our converts, that few missionary priests will care to dispense with its assistance."—*Register.* "It has very special merits of its own. . It is the work, not only of a thoughtful writer and good theologian, but of a wise and experienced priest."—*Dublin Review.* "Its characteristic is the singular simplicity and clearness with which everything is explained. . . It will save priests hours and days of time."—*Tablet.* "There is much in it with which we thoroughly agree."—*Church Times.* "There was a great want of a manual of instruction for convents, and the want has now been supplied, and in the most satisfactory manner."—*The Month.*

Descriptive Guide to the Mass. By the Rev. Dr. Laing. 1s. ; extra cloth, 1s. 6d.

"An attempt to exhibit the structure of the Mass. The logical relation of parts is ingeniously effected by an elaborate employment of differences of type, so that the classification, down to the minutest subdivision, may at once be caught by the eye."—*Tablet.*

Protestant Principles Examined by the Written Word. Originally entitled, "The Protestant's Trial by the Written Word." *New edition.* 18mo. 1s.

"An excellent book."—*Church News.* "A good specimen of the concise controversial writing of English Catholics in the early part of the seventeenth century."—*Catholic Opinion.* "A little book which might be consulted profitably by any Catholic."—*Church Times.* "A clever little manual."—*Westminster Gazette.* "A useful little volume."—*The Month.* "An excellent little book."—*Weekly Register.* "A well-written and well-argued treatise."—*Tablet.*

Fleury's Historical Catechism. Large edition, 1½d.

The Necessity of Enquiry as to Religion. By Henry John Pye, M.A. 4d. ; for distribution, 20s. a hundred ; cloth, 6d.

"Mr. Pye is particularly plain and straightforward."—*Tablet.* "It is calculated to do much good. We recommend it to the clergy, and think it a most useful work to place in the hands of all who are under instruction."—*Westminster Gazette.* "A thoroughly searching little pamphlet."—*Universe.* "A clever little pamphlet. Each point is treated briefly and clearly."—*Catholic Opinion.*

The Grounds of Catholic Doctrine. By Dr. Challoner. Large type edition. 18mo. cloth, 4d.

Dr. Butler's *First* Catechism, ½d. *Second* Catechism, 1d. ; *Third* Catechism, 1½d.

Dr. Doyle's Catechism, 1½d.

Lessons on the Christian Doctrine, 1d.

Bible History for the use of Catholic Schools and Families. By the Rev. R. Gilmour. 2s.

Herder's Prints—Old and New Testament. 40 large coloured pictures. 12s. *nett.*

Origin and Progress of Religious Orders, and Happiness of a Religious State. By Fr. Jerome Platus, S.J. ; translated by Patrick Mannock. Fcap. 8vo. 2s. 6d.

" The whole work is evidently calculated to impress any reader with the great advantages attached to a religious life."—*Register.*

Children of Mary in the World. 32mo. 1d.

Practical Counsels for Holy Communion. By Mgr. de Ségur. Translated for children, 1s.

Practical Counsels on Confession. By Mgr. de Ségur. Translated for children. 6d.

The Young Catholic's Guide to Confession and Holy Communion. By Dr. Kenny. *Third edition.* Paper, 4d. ; cloth, 6d. ; cloth, red edges, 9d.

" Admirably suited to the purpose for which it is intended."—*Weekly Register.* " One of the best we have seen. The instructions are clear, pointed, and devout, and the prayers simple, well constructed, and sufficiently brief. We recommend it to our readers." —*Church News.*

A General Catechism of the Christian Doctrine. By the Right Rev. Dr. Poirier. 18mo. 9d.

Explanation of the Epistles and Gospels, &c. By the Rev. Fr. Goffine. Illustrated. 7s.

Life, Passion, Death, and Resurrection of Our Blessed Lord. Translated from Ribadeneira. 1s.

Butler's Lives of the Saints. 2 vols., 8vo., cloth, 28s. ; or in cloth gilt, 34s. ; or in 4 vols., 8vo., cloth, 32s. ; or in cloth gilt, 48s. ; or in leather gilt, 64s.

Anglican Orders. By the Very Rev. Canon Williams. *Second Edition.* Crown 8vo. 3s. 6d.

Indulgences, Absolutions, &c. By Rev. Dr. Green. 4s, 6d.

Auricular Confession. By Rev. Dr. Melia. 1s. 6d.

The Rainy Day, and Guild of Our Lady. By the Rev. Fr. Richardson. 2d.

The Crusade, or Catholic Association for the Suppression of Drunkenness. By the Rev. Fr. Richardson. 1d.

Little by Little ; or, the Penny Bank. By the Rev. Fr. Richardson. 1d.

Temperance Tracts. No. 1. An Instructive and Interesting Dialogue. 1d.

A Letter to George Augustus Simcox, Esq. By One who has lately been received into the Church. 6d.

The Christian Teacher. By Ven. de la Salle. 1s. 8d.

Christian Politeness. By the Ven. de la Salle. 1s.

Duties of a Christian. By the Ven. de la Salle. 2s.

The Monks of Iona and the Duke of Argyll. By the Rev. J. Stewart M'Corry, D.D. 8vo. 3s. 6d.

Lives of Saints, &c.

Life of the Ven. Anna Maria Taigi. Translated from the French of Calixte, by A. V. Smith Sligo. 8vo. 5s.

"A most valuable book."—*Dublin Review.* "An edifying and delightful book of spiritual reading."—*Church Herald.* "We hope to see it meet with that success which works of the sort have a right to expect."—*Westminster Gazette.* "The translator's labour has been so ably performed that the book is wanting in few of the merits of an original work."—*Tablet.*

The Life of St. Francis of Assisi. Translated from the Italian of St. Bonaventure by Miss Lockhart. With a Preface by His Grace the Archbishop of Westminster. Fcap. 8vo. cloth, 2s. and 3s.; gilt, 4s.

"It is beautifully translated."—*Catholic Opinion.* "A most interesting and instructive volume."—*Tablet.* "This is a first-rate translation by one of the very few persons who have the art of translating as if they were writing an original work."—*Dublin Review.*

Oratorian Lives of the Saints. Second Series. Vol. I.—
    S. Bernardine of Siena.   Post 8vo. 5s.
    Vol. II.—S. Philip Benizi.   Post 8vo. 5s.
    Vol. III.—S. Veronica Giuliani, and Blessed
    Battista Varani.   Post 8vo. 5s.

1. It is proposed to publish a Second Series of the Lives of the Modern Saints, translated from foreign languages, and to bring out two or more volumes in the year. 2. The works translated from will be in most cases the Lives drawn up *for* or *from* the processes of canonization or beatification, as being more full, more authentic, and more replete with anecdote, thus enabling the reader to become better acquainted with the Saint's disposition and spirit ; while the simple matter-of-fact style of the narrative is, from its unobtrusive character, more adapted for spiritual reading than the views and generalizations, and prologetic extenuations of more recent biographers. 3. The objects are those stated at the commencement of the First Series, viz., 1. To supply English Catholics with a cabinet-library of interesting as well as edifying reading, especially for families, schools, and religious refectories, which would for many reasons be particularly adapted for these times, and would with God's blessing act as a counter influence to the necessarily deadening and chilling effects which the neighbourhood of heresy and the consequent prevalence of earthly principles and low views of grace may have on the temper and habits of mind even of the faithful ; 2. To present to our other countrymen a number of samples of the fruit which the system, doctrine, and moral discipline established by the holy and blessed Council of Trent have produced, and which will be to inquirers really in earnest about their souls, an argument more cogent than any that mere controversy can allege ; and 3. To spread the honour and love of the ever-blessed Queen of Saints, by showing how greatly an intense devotion to her aided in forming those prodigies of heroic virtue with which the Holy Ghost has been pleased to adorn the Church since the schism of Luther, *more than in almost any previous times ;* while the same motive will prevent the Series being confined to modern saints *exclusively.* 4. The work is published with the permission and approval of superiors. Every volume containing the Life of a person not yet canonized or beatified by the Church will be prefaced by a protest in conformity with the decree of Urban VIII., and in all Lives which introduce questions of mystical theology great care will be taken to publish nothing which has not had adequate sanction, or without the reader being informed of the nature and amount of the sanction.

Life of Fr. de Ravignan.   Crown 8vo. 9s.
The Pilgrimage to Paray le Monial, with a brief notice
    of the Blessed Margaret Mary.   6d.
Patron Saints.   By Eliza Allen Starr.   Cr. 8vo. 10s.

Life of St. Boniface, and the Conversion of Germany. By Mrs. Hope. Edited, with a Preface, by the Rev. Father Dalgairns. Cr. 8vo. 6s.

"Every one knows the story of S. Boniface's martyrdom, but every one has not heard it so stirringly set forth as in her 22nd chapter by Mrs. Hope."—*Dublin Review.*

Louise Lateau: her Life, Stigmata, and Ecstacies. By Dr. Lefebvre. Translated from the French by T. S. Shepard. Fcap. 8vo. 2s.; cheap edition, 6d.

Venerable Mary Christina of Savoy. 6d.

Memoirs of a Guardian Angel. Fcap. 8vo. 4s.

Life of St. Patrick. 12mo. 1s.

Life of St. Bridget, and of other Saints of Ireland. 1s.

Insula Sanctorum: the Island of Saints. 1s.; cloth, 2s.

Life of Paul Seigneret, Seminarist of Saint-Sulpice. Fcap. 8vo., 1s.; cloth extra, 1s. 6d.; gilt, 2s.

"An affecting and well-told narrative. . . It will be a great favourite, especially with our pure-minded, high-spirited young people." —*Universe.* "Paul Seigneret was remarkable for the simplicity and the heroism of both his natural and his religious character."—*Tablet.* "We commend it to parents with sons under their care, and especially do we recommend it to those who are charged with the education and training of our Catholic youth."—*Register.*

A Daughter of St. Dominic." By Grace Ramsay. Fcap. 8vo. 1s. 6d.; cloth extra, 2s.

"A beautiful little work. The narrative is highly interesting."— *Dublin Review.* "It is full of courage and faith and Catholic heroism."—*Universe.* "One who has lived and died in our own day, who led the common life of every one else, but yet who learned how to supernaturalize this life in so extraordinary a way that we forget 'the doctor's daughter in a provincial town,' while reading Grace Ramsay's beautiful picture of the wonders effected by her ubiquitous charity, and still more by her fervent prayer."—*Tablet.* "The spirit of thorough devotion to Rome manifest in every page of this charming work will render it most attractive to Leaguers of St. Sebastian."—*The Crusader.*

The Glory of St. Vincent de Paul. By the Most Rev. Dr. Manning, Archbishop of Westminster. 1s.

DR. NEWMAN'S LIVES OF THE ENGLISH SAINTS.

Life of St. Augustine of Canterbury. 12mo. 3s. 6d.

Life of St. German. 12mo. cloth, 3s. 6d.

Life of Stephen Langton. 12mo. cloth, 2s. 6d.

His Eminence Cardinal Wiseman ; with full account
   of his Obsequies ; Funeral Oration by Archbishop
   Manning, &c.   1s. ; cloth, red edges, 1s. 6d.
Count de Montalembert.   By George White.   6d.
Life of Mgr. Weedall.   By Dr. Husenbeth.   3s. 6d.
Life of Pope Pius IX.   6d.
Life of Rev. Fr. Pallotti.   By Rev. Dr. Melia.   4s.
   BY THE POOR CLARES OF KENMARE.
Life and Revelations of St. Gertrude.   Cr. 8vo.   7s. 6d.
Spirit of St. Gertrude.   18mo.   2s. 6d.
Life of St. Aloysius.   6d. ; St. Joseph, 6d., cloth, 9d. ;
   St. Patrick, 6d., cloth, 9d.
Life of St. Patrick.   Illustrated by Doyle.   4to. 20s.

Our Lady.

Life of the Ever-Blessed Virgin.   Proposed as a Model
   to Christian Women.   1s.
A May Chaplet, and other Verses for the Month of
   Mary.   Translated and Original.   By the Rev.
   Fr. Kenelm Digby Beste, of the Oratory.   With
   Imprimatur.   Square 16mo., cloth, 4s. ; gilt, 5s.
   " The Rev. Fr. Beste is the latest and not the least worthy singer
of the Virgin's praises.   Both as a translator and as an independent
composer, Fr. Beste's book is very laudable.   He is gifted with very
considerable pathetic power, and his style of expression is simple
and chaste.   His choice of metre is usually very happy, and the
melody of his verses leaves nothing to be desired.   But the great
charm of his volume is its manifest sincerity."—*Dublin Review.*
Our Blessed Lady of Lourdes: a Faithful Narrative of
   the Apparitions of the Blessed Virgin Mary at the
   Rocks of Massabielle, near Lourdes, in the year
   1858.   By F. C. Husenbeth, D.D., V.G., and Pro-
   vost of Northampton.   18mo. 6d. ; cloth 1s. :
   with Novena, 1s. ; cloth, 1s. 6d.   Novena, separately, 4d. ; Litany, separately, 1d.
Month of Mary for Interior Souls.   By M. A. Macdaniel.   18mo. 2s.
Concise Portrait of the Blessed Virgin.   1s. per 100.
The Definition of the Immaculate Conception.   6d.

Devotion to Our Lady in North America. By the Rev. Xavier Donald Macleod. 8vo. 5s. *cash.*

"The work of an author than whom few more gifted writers have ever appeared among us. It is not merely a religious work, but it has all the charms of an entertaining book of travels. We can hardly find words to express our high admiration of it."—*Weekly Register.*

The History of the Blessed Virgin. By the Abbé Orsini. Translated from the French by the Very Rev. F. C. Husenbeth, D.D. With eight Illustrations. Crown 8vo. 3s. 6d.

The Blessed Virgin's Root traced in the Tribe of Ephraim. By the Rev. Dr. Laing. 8vo. 10s. 6d.

Month of Mary, principally for the use of religious communities. 18mo. 1s. 6d.

Readings for the Feasts of Our Lady, and especially for the Month of May. By the Rev. A. P. Bethell. 18mo. 1s. 6d. ; cheap edition, 1s.

A Devout Exercise in Honour of the Blessed Virgin Mary. From the Psalter and Prayers of S. Bonaventure. In Latin and English, with Indulgences applicable to the Holy Souls. 32mo. 1s.

The Little Office of the Immaculate Conception. In Latin and English. By the Very Rev. Dr. Husenbeth. 32mo. 4d. ; cloth, 6d. ; roan, 1s.; calf or morocco, 2s. 6d.

Our Lady's Lament, and the Lamentation of St. Mary Magdalene. 2s.

Life of Our Lady in Verse. 2s.

The Virgin Mary. By Dr. Melia. 8vo. 11s. 3d. cash.

Archconfraternity of Our Lady of Angels. 1s. per 100.

Litany of Our Lady of Angels. 1s. per 100.

Origin of the Blue Scapular. 1d.

Prayer–Books.

Washbourne's Edition of the " Garden of the Soul," in medium-sized type (small type as a rule being avoided). For prices see page 4.

The Little Garden. 6d., 9d., 1s., 1s. 6d., and upwards.

The Lily of St. Joseph; a little Manual of Prayers and Hymns for Mass. Price 2d.; cloth, 3d.; or with gilt lettering, 4d.; more strongly bound, 6d.; or with gilt edges, 8d.; roan, 1s.; French morocco, 1s. 6d.; calf, or morocco, 2s.; gilt, 2s. 6d.

"It supplies a want which has long been felt; a prayer-book for children, which is not a childish book, a handy book for boys and girls, and for men and women too, if they wish for a short, easy-to-read, and devotional prayer-book."—*Catholic Opinion.* "A very complete prayer-book. It will be found very useful for children and for travellers."—*Weekly Register.* "A neat little compilation, which will be specially useful to our Catholic School-children. The hymns it contains are some of Fr. Faber's best."—*Universe.*

Life of Our Lord Commemorated in the Mass; a Method of Assisting at the Holy Sacrifice. By the Rev. E. G. Bagshawe, of the Oratory. 32mo. 3d.; cloth, 4d.; roan, 1s.; French morocco, 1s. 6d.; calf or morocco, 2s. 6d.

Garden of the Soul, in large type. Roan, gilt edges, 2s.; French morocco, 3s., clasp and rims, 4s. 6d.; French morocco, antique, 3s. 6d.; calf, 5s.; morocco, 6s. 6d.; roan, sprinkled edges, with Epistles and Gospels, 2s. All the other styles with Epistles and Gospels, 6d. extra.

Path to Paradise. 36 full page Illustrations. Cloth, 3d. With 50 Illustrations, cloth, 4d.

Manual of Catholic Devotion. Small, for the waist-coat pocket. 6d.; roan, 1s.; calf or morocco, 2s.

Ursuline Manual. Persian calf, 7s. 6d.; morocco, 10s.

Crown of Jesus. Persian calf, 6s.; morocco, 7s. 6d. and 8s. 6d., with rims, 10s. 6d.; morocco, extra gilt, 10s. 6d., with rims, 12s. 6d.; ivory, with rims, 21s., 25s., 27s. 6d. and 30s.

Burial of the Dead (Adults and Infants) in Latin and English. Royal 32mo. cloth, 6d.; roan, 1s. 6d.

"Being in a portable form, will be found useful by those who are called upon to assist at that solemn rite."—*Tablet.*

In Suffragiis Sanctorum. Commem S. Josephi. Commem S. Georgii. Set of five for 4d.

Sacred Heart of Jesus offered to the Piety of the Young engaged in Study. By Rev. A. Deham, S.J. 6d.
"Complete little Manual of Devotion to the Sacred Heart, and as such will be valued by Catholics of every age and station."—*Tablet.*

Treasury of the Sacred Heart. With Epistles and Gospels. 18mo. cloth, 3s. 6d. ; roan, 4s. 6d.

Little Treasury of the Sacred Heart. 32mo. 2s.

Devotions to Sacred Heart of Jesus. By the Rt. Rev. Dr. Milner. *New Edition.* To which is added Devotions to the Immaculate Heart of Mary. 3d. ; cloth, 6d. ; gilt, 1s.

Manual of Devotion to the Sacred Heart, from the Writings of Bl. Margaret Mary Alacoque. By Denys Casassayas. Translated. 3d.

Act of Consecration to the Sacred Heart. 1d.

Act of Reparation to the Sacred Heart. 1s. per 100.

The Little Prayer-Book for Ordinary Catholic Devotions. Cloth, 3d.

Missal (complete). Persian calf, 8s. 6d. ; morocco, 10s. 6d., with rims, 13s. 6d. ; morocco, extra gilt, 12s. 6d., with rims, 15s. 6d. ; morocco, with turnover edges, 13s. 6d.; morocco antique, 15s. ; russia antique, 20s. ; ivory, with rims, 31s. 6d.

Manual of Catholic Piety, containing a selection of Fervent Prayers, Pious Reflections, and Solid Instructions, adapted to every State of Life. Edition with green border. French mor., 2s. 6d.; mor., 4s.

Occasional Prayers for Festivals. By Rev. T. Barge. 32mo. 4d. and 6d. ; gilt, 1s.

Catholic Hours : a Manual of Prayer, including Mass and Vespers. By J. R. Digby Beste, Esq. 32mo. cloth, 2s; red edges, 2s. 6d.; roan, 3s.; morocco, 6s.

Catholic Piety. 32mo. 6d.; roan, 1s. ; with Epistles and Gospels, roan, 1s. ; French morocco, 1s. 6d., with rims and clasp, 2s. ; imitation ivory, rims and clasp, 2s. 6d. ; velvet rims and clasps, 3s. 6d.

Key of Heaven. Same size and prices.

Manual of Devotions in Honour of Our Lady of Sorrows. Compiled by the Clergy at St. Patrick's Soho. 18mo. 1s. ; cloth, red edges, 1s. 6d.

Novena to St. Joseph. Translated by M. A. Macdaniel. To which is added a Pastoral of the late Right Rev. Dr. Grant. 32mo. 4d. ; cloth, 6d.

"All seasons are fitting in which to make Novenas to St. Joseph, for which reason this little work will be found very serviceable at any time."—*Weekly Register.*

Miraculous Prayer—August Queen of Angels. 1s. per 100.

A Union of our life with the Passion of our Lord, by a daily offering. 1s. per 100.

A New Year's Gift to our Heavenly Father ; or, Dedication of the First Hours of the Year, Quarter, Month, or Week to God. 4d.

Devotions for Mass. Very large type, 2d.

Memorare Mass. By the Poor Clares of Kenmare, 2d

Fourteen Stations of the Holy Way of the Cross. By St. Liguori. Large type edition, 1d.

Prayer for one's Confessor. 1s. per 100.

Litany of Resignation. 1s. per 100.

Intentions for Indulgences. 6d. per 100.

Prayers for the Dying. 1s. per 100.

Indulgenced Prayers for the Rosary of the Ho Souls. 1d. each, 6d. a dozen, 3s. per 100.

Indulgenced Prayers for Souls in Purgatory. 1s. per 1'

Devotions to St. Joseph. 1s. per 100.

Devotion to St. Joseph as Patron of the Church.

Catholic Piety, or Key of Heaven, with Epistles Gospels. Large 32mo, French morocco, with rims, 2s. 6d. ; extra gilt, 3s. ; with rims, 3s.

Douai Bible. 2s. 6d. ; calf or morocco, 6s. ; gilt,

Catholic Psalmist : or, Manual of Sacred Music, taining Vespers, Chants, Hymns, Litanies, with the Gregorian Chants for High Mass, Week, &c. Compiled by C. B. Lyons, 4s.

The Complete Hymn Book, containing 136 Hymns
for Missions, Month of Mary. Price 1d.

Church Hymns. By J. R. Digby Beste, Esq. 6d.

Illustrated Manual of Prayers. 32mo., 3d. ; cloth, 4d.

Key of Heaven. Very large type, 1s. Leather 2s. 6d. gilt, 3s.

Catholic Choir Manual : containing Vespers for all
the Sundays and Festivals of the year, Hymns and
Litanies, &c. Compiled by C. B. Lyons. 1s.

The Rosary for the Souls in Purgatory, *with Indulgenced Prayer.* 6d. and 9d. each. Medals separately, 1d. each, 9s. gross. Prayers separately, 1d.
each, 3s. per 100.

Rome, &c.

Two Years in the Pontifical Zouaves. By Joseph
Powell, Z.P. With 4 Engravings by Sergeant
Collingridge, Z.P. 8vo. 3s. 6d.

" It affords us much pleasure, and deserves the notice of the Catholic public."—*Tablet.* " Familiar names meet the eye on every page,
and as few Catholic circles in either country have not had a friend or
relative at one time or another serving in the Pontifical Zouaves, the
history of the formation of the corps, of the gallant youths, their
sufferings, and their troubles, will be valued as something more than
a contribution to modern Roman history."—*Freeman's Journal.*

The Victories of Rome. By the Rev. Fr. Kenelm
Digby Beste. Second edition. 1s.

The Roman Question. By F. C. Husenbeth, D.D. 1s.

Defence of the Roman Church against Fr. Gratry.
By Dom Gueranger. 6d.

Personal Recollections of Rome. By W. J. Jacob,
Esq., late of the Pontifical Zouaves. 8vo. 1s. 6d.

Henri V. (Comte de Chambord), September 29, 1873.
By W. H. Walsh. With a Portrait. 8vo. 1s. 6d.

The Rule of the Pope-King. By Rev. Fr. Martin. 6d.

The Years of Peter. By an Ex-Papal Zouave. 1d.

The Catechism of the Council. By a D.C.L. 2d.

The Crucifixion. Coloured, on black ground. Size
20in. by 27in. Price 2s.

Tales, or Books for the Library.

Tom's Crucifix, and other Tales. By M. F. S.   3s.

"Eight simple stories for the use of teachers of Christian doctrine."—*Universe.* "This is a volume of short, plain, and simple stories, written with the view of illustrating the Catholic religion practically by putting Catholic practices in an interesting light before the mental eyes of children....The whole of the tales in the volume before us are exceedingly well written."—*Register.*

Simple Tales.   Square 16mo. cloth antique, 2s. 6d.

"Contains five pretty stories of a true Catholic tone, interspersed with some short pieces of poetry. . . Are very affecting, and told in such a way as to engage the attention of any child."—*Register.* "This is a little book which we can recommend with great confidence as a present for young readers. The tales are simple, beautiful, and pathetic."—*Catholic Opinion.* "It belongs to a class of books of which the want is generally much felt by Catholic parents." —*Dublin Review.* "Beautifully written. 'Little Terence' is a gem of a Tale."—*Tablet.*

Fairy Tales for Little Children. By Madeleine Howley
    Meehan.   Fcap. 1s. ; cloth extra, 1s. 6d.; gilt, 2s.

"Full of imagination and dreams, and at the same time with excellent point and practical aim, within the reach of the intelligence of infants."—*Universe.* "Pleasing, simple stories, combining instruction with amusement."—*Register.* "A pretty little story-book for pretty little children."—*Tablet.*

Terry O'Flinn's Examination of Conscience. By the
    Very Rev. Dr. Tandy.   Fcap. 8vo. 1s. 6d. ;
    extra gilt, 2s. ; cheap edition, 1s.

"The writer possesses considerable literary power."—*Register.* "The idea is well sustained throughout, and when the reader comes to the end of the book he finds the mystery solved, and that it was all nothing but a 'dhrame.'"—*Church Times.*

The Adventures of a Protestant in Search of a Reli-
    gion : being the Story of a late Student of
    Divinity at Bunyan Baptist College ; a Noncon-
    formist Minister, who seceded to the Catholic
    Church.   By Iota.   5s. ; cheap edition, 3s.

"Will well repay its perusal."—*Universe.* "This precious volume."—*Baptist.* "No one will deny 'Iota' the merit of entire originality."—*Civilian.* "A valuable addition to every Catholic library." *Tablet.* "There is much cleverness in it."—*Nonconformist.* "Malicious and wicked."—*English Independent.*

The Fisherman's Daughter. By Conscience.   4s.

The Amulet. By Hendrick Conscience. 4s.

Rosalie ; or, the Memoirs of a French Child. Written by herself. Fcap. 8vo., 1s. and 1s. 6d. ; extra gilt, 2s.

"It is prettily told, and in a natural manner. The account of Rosalie's illness and First Communion is very well related. We can recommend the book for the reading of children."—*Tablet.* "The tenth chapter is beautiful."—*Universe.*

The Story of Marie and other Tales. Fcap. 8vo., 2s.; cloth extra, 2s. 6d.; gilt, 3s.; or separately:—The Story of Marie, 2d.; Nelly Blane, and A Contrast, 2d.; A Conversion and a Death-Bed, 2d.; Herbert Montagu, 2d. ; Jane Murphy, The Dying Gipsy, and The Nameless Grave, 2d.; The Beggars, and True and False Riches, 2d.; Pat and his Friend, 2d.

"A very nice little collection of stories, thoroughly Catholic in their teaching."—*Tablet.* "A series of short pretty stories, told with much simplicity."—*Universe.* ' A number of short pretty stories, replete with religious teaching, told in simple language."— *Weekly Register.*

Margarethe Verflassen. Translated from the German by Mrs. Smith Sligo. Fcap. 8vo. 3s. ; gilt, 3s. 6d.

"A portrait of a very holy and noble soul, whose life was passed in constant practical acts of the love of God."—*Weekly Register.* "It is the picture of a true woman's life, well fitted up with the practice of ascetic devotion and loving unwearied activity about all the works of mercy."—*Tablet.*

The Last of the Catholic O'Malleys. A Tale. By M. Taunton. 18mo. cloth, 1s. 6d. ; extra, 2s.

"A sad and stirring tale, simply written, and sure to secure for itself readers."—*Tablet.* "Deeply interesting. It is well adapted for parochial and school libraries."—*Weekly Register.* "A very pleasing tale."—*The Month.*

Eagle and Dove. From the French of Mademoiselle Zénaïde Fleuriot. By Emily Bowles. Cr. 8vo., 5s.

"We recommend our readers to peruse this well-written story."— *Register.* "One of the very best stories we have ever dipped into." —*Church Times.* "Admirable in tone and purpose."—*Church Herald.* "A real gain. It possesses merits far above the pretty fictions got up by English writers."—*Dublin Review.* "There is an air of truth and sobriety about this little volume, nor is there any attempt at sensation."—*Tablet.*

Rupert Aubray. By the Rev. T. J. Potter. 3s.

Farleyes of Farleye. By the same author. 2s. 6d.

Sir Humphrey's Trial. By the same author. 2s. 6d.

R. Washbourne, 18 *Paternoster Row, London.*

Chats about the Rosary; or, Aunt Margaret's Little Neighbours. Fcap. 8vo. 3s.

"There is scarcely any devotion so calculated as the Rosary to keep up a taste for piety in little children, and we must be grateful for any help in applying its lessons to the daily life of those who already love it in their unconscious tribute to its value and beauty." —*Month.* "We do not know of a better book for reading aloud to children, it will teach them to understand and to love the Rosary."— *Tablet.* "A graceful little book, in fifteen chapters, on the Rosary, illustrative of each of the mysteries, and connecting each with the practice of some particular virtue."—*Catholic Opinion.*

Cistercian Legends of the 13th Century. Translated from the Latin by the Rev. Henry Collins. 3s.

Cloister Legends: or, Convents and Monasteries in the Olden Time. *Second Edition.* Cr. 8vo. 4s.

The People's Martyr, a Legend of Canterbury. 4s.

Keighley Hall and other Tales. By Elizabeth King. 18mo. 6d.; cloth, 1s.; gilt, 1s. 6d.; or, separately, Keighley Hall, Clouds and Sunshine, The Maltese Cross, 3d. each.

Sir Ælfric and other Tales. By the Rev. G. Bampfield. 18mo. 6d.; cloth, 1s.; gilt, 1s. 6d.

Ned Rusheen. By the Poor Clares. Crown 8vo. 6s.

The Prussian Spy. A Novel. By V. Valmont. 4s.

Adolphus; or, the Good Son. 18mo. gilt, 6d.

Nicholas; or, the Reward of a Good Action. 6d.

The Lost Children of Mount St. Bernard. 18mo. gilt, 6d.

A Broken Chain. 18mo. gilt, 6d.

The Baker's Boy; or, the Results of Industry. 6d.

"All prettily got up, artistically illustrated, and pleasantly-written. Better books for gifts and rewards we do not know."— *Weekly Register.* "We can thoroughly recommend them."—*Tablet.*

The Truce of God: a Tale of the Eleventh Century. By G. H. Miles. 4s.

Tales and Sketches. By Charles Fleet. 8vo. cloth, 2s. and 2s. 6d.; cloth, gilt, 3s. 6d.

"Pleasingly-written, and containing some valuable hints. There is a good deal of nice feeling in these short stories."—*Tablet.*

The Convent Prize Book. By the author of "Geraldine." Fcap. 8vo. 2s. 6d.; gilt, 3s. 6d.

The Journey of Sophia and Eulalie to the Palace of True Happiness. Translated by the Rev. Father Ambrose, Mount St. Bernard's. Fcap. 8vo. 3s. 6d. ; cheap edition, 2s. 6d.

Florence O'Neill. By A. M. Stewart. 4s. 6d. and 6s.

Limerick Veteran. By the same. 4s. 6d. and 6s.

The Three Elizabeths. By the same. 3s. 6d. and 4s.6d.

Alone in the World. By the same. 3s. 6d. and 4s. 6d.

Festival Tales. By J. F. Waller. 5s.

Shakespeare's Plays and Tragedies. Abridged and Revised for the use of Schools. By Rosa Baughan. 8vo. 7s. 6d.

Poems. By H. N. Oxenham. *Third Edition.* 3s. 6d.

Miscellaneous and Educational.

History of Modern Europe. With a Preface by the Right Rev. Dr. Weathers. 12mo. cloth, 5s.; gilt, 6s. ; roan, 5s. 6d.

" A work of especial importance for the way in which it deals with the early part of the present Pontificate."—*Weekly Register.*

Culpepper. An entirely New Edition of Brook's Family Herbal. 150 engravings, drawn and coloured from living specimens. Crown 8vo., 5s. 6d.

The Continental Fish Cook; or, a Few Hints on Maigre Dinners. By M. J. N. de Frederic. 18mo. 1s.

" This is an admirable collection of recipes, which many house-keepers will welcome for use. We strongly recommend our lady readers at once to procure it."—*Church Herald.* " It will give to all mistresses of households very valuable hints on maigre dinners, and we feel sure they will be glad to know of the existence of such a manual."—*Register.* " There are 103 recipes, all of which have been practically tested ; they combine variety, wholesomeness, and economy."—*Universe.* " It is an unpretending little work, but nevertheless containing many recipes, enabling housekeepers to pro-vide an excellent variety of dishes, such as may lawfully be eaten in times of fasting and abstinence."—*Church Times.*

On the Spirit in which Scientific Studies should be pursued, with Remarks on the Darwinian Theory of Evolution. By Mr. George Richardson. 8vo. 6d.

General Questions in History, Chronology, Geogra-phy, the Arts, &c. By A. M. Stewart. 4s. 6d.

Elements of Philosophy, comprising Logic, and
    General Principles of Metaphysics. By Rev. W.
    H. Hill, S.J.   Second edition, 8vo. 6s.

"This work is from the pen of one who has devoted many years to
the study and teaching of philosophy. It is elementary, and must
be concise; yet it treats the important points of philosophy so
clearly, and contains so many principles of wide application, that it
cannot fail to be especially useful in a country where sound philo-
sophical doctrine is perhaps more needed than in any other."

University Education, under the Guidance of the
    Church; or, Monastic Studies.   By a Monk of St.
    Augustine's, Ramsgate.   8vo. 2s. 6d.

"An admirable pamphlet. Its contents are above praise. We
trust that it will be widely circulated."—*Weekly Register.* "The
author is evidently a scholar, a well-read man, and a person of experience and wide reading. His essay, consequently, is worth both
studying and preserving."—*Church Herald.*

History of England. By W. Mylius. 12mo. 3s. 6d.
Catechism of the History of England. Cloth, 1s.
History of Ireland. By T. Young. 18mo. cloth, 2s. 6d.
The Illustrated History of Ireland. By the Nun of
    Kenmare.   Illustrated by Doyle. 8vo. 11s.
The Patriots' History of Ireland.   By the Poor Clares
    of Kenmare.   18mo. cloth, 2s. ; cloth gilt, 2s. 6d.
A Chronological Sketch of the Kings of England and
    France.   With Anecdotes for the use of Children.
    By H. Murray Lane. 2s. 6d. ; or separately,
*   England, 1s. 6d., France, 1s. 6d.

"Admirably adapted for teaching young children the elements of
English and French history."—*Tablet.* "A very useful little pub-
lication."—*Weekly Register.* "An admirably arranged little work
for the use of children."—*Universe.*

The Catholic Alphabet of Scripture Subjects.   Price,
    on a sheet, plain, 1s. ; coloured, 2s. ; mounted
    on linen, to fold in a case, 3s. 6d. ; varnished, on
    linen, on rollers, 4s.

"This will be hailed with joy by all young children in Catholic
schools, and we should gladly see it placed conspicuously before the
eyes of our little ones."—*Catholic Opinion.* "Will be very welcome
in the infant school."—*Weekly Register.*

Bell's Modern Reader and Speaker.   Cloth, 3s. 6d.

Extracts from the Fathers and other Writers of the Church. 12mo. cloth, 4s. 6d.

Brickley's Standard Table Book, ½d.

Washbourne's Multiplication Table on a sheet, 3s. per 100. Specimen sent for 1d. stamp.

Music.

BY HERR WILHELM SCHULTHES.

Cor Jesu, Salus in Te Sperantium. 4s. for 2s.; with harp accompaniment, 5s. for 2s. 6d.; abridged edition, 3d.

Mass of the Holy Child Jesus, and Ave Maria for unison and congregational singing, with organ accompaniment. 6s. for 3s.

The Vocal Part may be had separately, in 18mo., at 4d. each, or 22s. 6d. cash per 100; or bound in cloth, at 6d. each, or 33s. 6d. cash per 100.

The Ave Maria of this Mass can be had for Four Voices, with the Ingressus Angelus. 2s. 6d. for 1s. 3d.

Recordare. Oratio Jeremiæ Prophetæ. 2s. for 1s.

Ne projicias me a facie Tua. Motett for Four Voices. (T.B.) 2s. 6d. for 1s. 3d.

Benediction Service, with 36 Litanies. 12s. for 6s.

Oratory Hymns. 2 vols., folio, 16s. for 8s.

Regina Cœli. Motett for Four Voices. 6s. for 3s.; vocal arrangement, 2s. for 1s.

Twelve Latin Hymns, for Vespers, &c. 2s.

Portfolio. With a patent metallic back. 3s.

Litanies. By Rev. J. McCarthy. 2s. 6d. for 1s. 3d.

Six Litany Chants. By F. Leslie. 6d.

Ave Maria. By T. Haydn Waud. 3s. for 1s. 6d.

Fr. Faber's Hymns. Various, 1s. 6d. for 9d. each.

A separate Catalogue of FOREIGN Books, Educational Books, Books for the Library or for Prizes, supplied ; also a Catalogue of School and General Stationery, a Catalogue of Second-hand Books, and a Catalogue of Crucifixes and other Religious Articles.

INDEX TO AUTHORS.

CONTENTS.

R. WASHBOURNE, 18 PATERNOSTER ROW.